Tough Love

Skye Warren

CHAPTER ONE

THE MOON SITS high above the tree line. Somewhere beyond those woods is an electric fence. And beyond that is an entire city of people living and working and *loving* each other. I may as well be on the moon for how close I am to them.

A guard walks by my window at 10:05 p.m. Right on time.

I wait a few minutes until he's out of earshot; then I flip the latch. From there it's quick work to push up the pane with its bulletproof glass. I broke the lock a year ago. And almost every night since then I've sneaked down the ornate metal trellis—like a thief, stealing a moment to myself.

The grass is still damp from the rain, the ground beneath like a sponge, sucking me in. I cross the lawn, heart beating against my chest. I know exactly where the guards are on their rounds. I know exactly where the trip wires are that will set off the alarms. My father is too busy in his office to even glance outside.

The office I broke into this morning.

I breathe a sigh of relief when I reach the pool. I'm still out in the open, but the bright underwater lights make it hard to see anything on the patio. They make it hard to see me as I curve around the edge and reach the pool house.

The door opens before I touch the handle. "Clara," comes the whisper.

I can't help but smile as I slip into the dark. Giovanni always opens the door for me. It's like some old-world chivalry thing, even though we're just two kids sneaking around. At least, that's how everyone treats me. Like a kid. But when I'm with him, I feel less like a girl, more like a woman.

He looks out the door for a beat before shutting and locking it. "Are you sure no one saw you?"

"You're such a worrywart, Gio." I let myself fall onto the couch, facing up.

"If your father ever found out…"

We'd be in so much trouble. My father is a member of the mob. Giovanni's father is a foot soldier who works security on the grounds. Both our dads are seriously dangerous, not to mention a little unhinged. I can't even think about how bad it would be if they caught us sneaking around after dark.

I push those thoughts away. "Did you bring it?"

Reluctantly, Giovanni nods. He gestures to the side table, where a half-full bottle of Jack Daniels gleams in the faint light. "Did you?"

I reach into the pockets of my jeans and pull out two cigars. I hold them up and grin. "Didn't even break a sweat."

He rolls his eyes, but I think he's relieved. "This was a bad idea."

"It was my idea," I remind him, and his cheeks turn dark.

Of course the little homework assignment was my idea. I'm the one ridiculously sheltered up in my room with the tutors and the gilded locks. Fifteen years old and I've never even been out to the movies. Giovanni gets to go to regular school. He's too young to get inducted, but I know he gets to be at some of the sit-ins.

"I just want to try them," I say. "I'm not going to get addicted or anything."

He snorts. "More likely you'll get a hangover. How are you going to explain puking to your padre?"

"Honor will cover for me." My sister always covers for me. She takes the brunt of my father's anger. Ninety-nine percent of the time, I love the way she protects me. But one percent of the time, it feels like a straitjacket. That's why I started coming to the pool house. And I'm glad I did. This is where I met Giovanni.

He examines the cigar, eyes narrowed.

"How do you even light it?" I ask. I've seen my father do it a hundred times, but I'm still not clear on how the whole thing doesn't just catch fire. Isn't it made from dried plants?

He puts the cigar to his lips experimentally. It looks strange seeing his full lips around something I've mostly seen my father use. Then he blows out a breath, miming how it would be. I imagine white smoke curling in front of his tanned skin.

"They don't let you use them when they do?" I ask.

He gives me a dark look. I'm not supposed to talk about the side jobs he does for his father. "I mostly sit in a corner and hope no one notices me. It's boring."

"If it's boring, then why won't you talk about it?" I know it's not a good thing to be noticed by men like our father, to be groomed by them, but sometimes that seems better than being ignored. I'm the younger one. And a girl. And there are rumors that I'm not even my father's legitimate child. In other words, I'm lucky my sister remembers to feed me.

He swears in Italian. "That's no life for you, Clara."

"And it's a life for you?"

"I would leave if I could," he says. "You know that."

"You turn eighteen in a year. Will you leave then?" My stomach clenches at the thought of him gone. I'm two years younger than him. And even when I turn eighteen, I won't be leaving. By then I'll be engaged to whoever my father picks for me.

Just like my sister. I shudder at the thought of her fiancé.

He shrugs. "We'll see."

I roll my eyes. I suspect he's making plans, but he isn't sharing them with me. That's how the men around here operate, keeping girls in the dark. Honor only found out she was engaged when Byron was invited over for dinner. He has the money and the power. She doesn't get a choice. Neither will I.

"If you go, you should take me with you," I say.

"I don't think Honor would appreciate me taking you away."

No, she wouldn't. And the thought of being without my sister makes my heart ache. Sometimes I give her a hard time, but I love her. I'd never leave her behind. "She can come with us. It will be like an adventure."

"Don't talk stupid, Clara." His eyes flash with anger and something else I can't define.

I jerk back, hurt. "It was just an idea."

"Well, it's a bad idea. Your father is never gonna let you leave."

Deep inside, I turn cold. I know that's true. Of course it is. Giovanni doesn't have the money or the resources to take us away from here. And even if he did, why would he want to?

I hate myself for even suggesting it. How desperate can I look?

Shaking inside, I stand up and grab the bottle of Jack Daniels. It's heavier than I would have expected, but I carry it over to a wet bar still stocked with decanters and wine glasses. No liquor though. There used to be huge parties here. When my mother died, they stopped.

We're supposed to have a party in a few days, though, to celebrate my sister's engagement. I'm not even allowed to go. I'll just be able to see the fireworks from the window.

Without a word Giovanni joins me, his heat both comforting and stark. He takes the glass from my shaking hand. He opens the bottle and pours the deep amber liquid inside. Then takes another cup for himself, twice as full.

"Why do you get more?" I protest, mostly because I like teasing him.

His expression is amused. "I'm bigger than you."

He is bigger. Taller and broader, though still skinny. His hands are bigger than mine too. They hold the glass with confidence, whereas I almost drop mine.

I take a sip before I can second-guess myself. "*Oh my God.*"

It burns my throat, battery acid scalding me all the way down.

His lips firm, like he's trying not to laugh. "Good stuff?"

"Oh, shut up." Then it doesn't matter because I'm laughing too. That stuff is *awful.*

He grins and takes a drink—more like a gulp. And he doesn't cough or wince after. "You get used to it."

"How much do I have to drink to get used to it?"

"More than you should."

I take another sip. It burns again, but I have to say, not as bad. It still doesn't taste good, but I'm determined to drink it anyway. This pool house is the only place where I can break the rules, where I can experience things. The pool house is the only place I even feel alive.

"Let's try mine," I say. My voice already sounds rougher from the alcohol.

He holds up the cigar. "Did you bring a lighter?"

"Oh, crap."

His eyes crinkle in that way I love. It makes my chest feel full, like there's no room for air. "It doesn't matter," he says.

"But I didn't hold up my end of the bargain."

He takes another drink. It looks so natural when he does it. "What bargain?"

"To do bad things," I say seriously. When your life is as controlled as mine, you need to plan these things. Tonight is supposed to be the night.

He looks down, a strange smile on his face. "Let's start with the whiskey. If that's not enough, we can knock over a bank or something."

I smack his arm. "You're making fun of me."

"Never." His eyes meet mine, and I see that he's not laughing at all. "I'd rob a bank if you wanted me to."

My stomach twists at his solemn tone. "I'd rather you stay safe," I whisper.

He reaches a hand toward me like he's going to cup my face, only half an inch away he freezes. I can almost feel the heat of him, and I remain very still, waiting to see what he'll do next.

He shoves his empty glass onto the bar and walks away.

I let out a breath. What is that about? Lately we keep having these moments where it seems, like he's going to touch me. But he never does. I want to touch him too, but I don't. I wouldn't know where to start. I can't even imagine how he'd feel. Would he be like the whiskey, leaving a trail of fire? I'm scared to find out.

He's on the couch, so I join him there. Not touching, just sitting beside him.

"Gio, I'm worried about Honor."

He doesn't look at me. "She's strong. She can take care of herself."

"Yeah, but Byron is a jerk." And even she can't fight the tides. That's what men like Byron are. Tsunamis. Hurricanes. Natural disasters.

"Your dad wants someone who can take over. That's pretty much guaranteed to be an asshole."

He's not saying anything I don't know, but it's still frustrating. It's too dark to see his expression. I can only see the shape of him beside me, his neck and shoulders limned by moonlight. "This isn't the eighteenth century. This is Las Vegas."

"Marriage isn't about that. Not here."

It's about making alliances. It's about *money.* "He should make *you* the next one in line."

At least Gio has been around for years. His dad is trusted here, even if he's not high ranking. This Byron guy hasn't even been in Las Vegas very long. And he's a cop. I learned from an early age not to trust cops—even dirty ones.

Gio shakes his head. "No, thanks."

"Why not? You'd be good at it." I can tell he's biting his tongue. "What?"

"Good at killing people?" he asks softly.

I flinch. Most of the time we skirt around what exactly my father does. And technically Gio is a part of that. I've never asked him if he's killed someone. For all I know, he already has robbed a bank. He's still in high school, so they're keeping him light. But once he graduates high school, they'll want to induct him. I'd almost rather he did leave then. Even though it would kill me to see him go.

He shakes his head. "Anyway, if it were me being groomed, I'd have to marry Honor. And I couldn't do that."

The thought of him marrying my sister makes my stomach knot. He's only a couple years younger than her. It's actually not a bad idea. "Why not?"

"Because I like her sister."

I go very still. There's only one sister. *Me.*

"What did you say?" I whisper.

"You heard me." He leans close. He reaches for me— and this time, his hand does cup my cheek. The feel of him is shocking, startling, impossibly coarse and warm at the same time. He runs his thumb along my skin, rasping against me. My eyes flutter closed.

The old leather of the couch creaks as he leans forward. He must be inches away now. His breath coasts over my lips. Goose bumps rise on my skin. I'm waiting…hoping…

Suddenly his lips are against mine, warm and soft. God, I've seen those lips smile and twist and curse a blue streak, but I never imagined they could be this soft. Nothing like whiskey, with its fire. This is a gentle heat, a caress, and I sink into him, let myself go lax.

One second later, he's gone. Not touching me at all.

My eyes snap open. "Gio?"

He looks tormented. I may not have felt the whiskey burn, but he did. Pain flashes through his eyes. He stands and walks away. "No, Clara. That was wrong. I was wrong to do that."

"But why?" How could that be wrong? That was the best thing that ever happened to me. On a night when I wanted to be *bad,* I experienced my first kiss. It's the best bad thing I could have imagined. And it tasted so sweet.

He's still shaking his head, so vehemently I'm not sure who he's trying to convince—me or himself. "You've been drinking."

"One drink," I say, kind of insulted. I may be new to this, but I'm not drunk.

"One drink is enough."

"You had one drink too," I point out, accusing.

He laughs, the sound unsteady and harsh. "I'm bigger than you."

I don't know if he means the drink affects him less or if it's just another reason why the kiss was a bad idea—as if he might have overpowered me. But there is no reason why this is a bad idea. I've wanted him to kiss me forever. And judging by the way he kissed just now, he liked it too. Unless…

My voice is small. "Did I…do it wrong?"

He lets out a string of curse words. "No, *bella.* You did nothing wrong. This is me. I can't touch you when you've been drinking. I can't touch you at all."

CHAPTER TWO

I GROAN AS light batters my eyelids. There's sound too. And something heavy pressing down on my head. I flutter my hand in the universal sign for *go away*. In case that wasn't clear enough, I add, "Turn off the light."

"That's the sun, silly," my sister says.

I peek one eye open and am totally blinded. If that's the sun, we must be going through some kind of apocalypse, because it's a hundred times brighter than I've ever seen it. And since when did she speak through a microphone? All I manage to do is whimper.

The bed dips as she sits down next to me. Her hand is cool and dry against my forehead. "Are you sick or something? You don't look that great."

"Thanks," I say wryly and then wince as the word echoes through my head.

Last night comes back to me with a crash. The Jack Daniels. Then the *kiss*. Then rejection.

Then more Jack Daniels.

We finished the whole bottle while very pointedly not discussing kissing. "I'm not sick," I tell her so at least she won't worry. Even though I feel worse than when I had the flu. I hope a hangover doesn't last for days.

"I'll take your temperature," she says, heading toward the bathroom connected to my room.

"No," I protest. The thought of something beeping in my ear makes me cringe. I force myself to sit up, to prove I'm okay. "See? I'm fine."

Honor is wearing a cream vintage blouse and black pencil skirt. She always looks so put together. I glance at the clock. Ten o'clock in the morning. Okay, I guess it's not that early. Still, she looks classy and stylish at any hour of the day. Her expression is tight. Because of me?

"I'm fine," I repeat.

The line of worry between her eyes fades, but her lips are still pressed together. There's something about her expression that's familiar. Then I realize… it's pain. Real pain. Not the kind of throbbing ache I'm experiencing now, an ache I completely deserve. This is something else.

I stand and approach her.

"We're meeting with the caterer in thirty minutes," she says. She's letting me sit in on the planning sessions so I can feel involved. The food, the cake. The fireworks.

Kind of crazy, having fireworks in the middle of a freaking drought. That's the benefit of having the fire inspector in your pocket. Or Byron's pocket.

Gently, I take her arm. I press the sheer fabric against her skin—and with the fabric taut, I can see. There they are, three bruises. "Did Byron do this to you?"

She pulls away. "I don't know what you're talking about."

I roll my eyes. "Maybe that works on other people, but not me. I'm going to go punch him in the face."

She looks alarmed, even though the punching thing is pretty unlikely. I'm not even tall enough. And he'd probably shoot me. I don't mind telling him off, though. He can't shoot me for that.

"Stay away from him," she warns.

"Or what? He'll grab me too? He probably hurts you other places, doesn't he? Places I can't even see."

She shakes her head even though I know it's true. She's not even really denying it. She's saying *leave it alone*. "Anything you do will just make it worse."

I hate that she's right about that. "Then we'll talk to Daddy. He can make him stop."

Pain flashes over Honor's face. "He already knows."

My eyes close. I'd been afraid of that. Afraid that Byron's connections and money were worth seeing my sister hurt. Byron may be relatively new to the scene, but he's ambitious. And like Brutus, an ambitious man is a dangerous one. He has money and connections. My father is old and growing weaker. The other factions could see it as an opportunity to take over. So he's solidified his rule by grooming Byron to take over—and marrying his oldest daughter to him as insurance.

I swallow hard. Our father never took much interest in me. Maybe the rumors are true and I'm not really his daughter. I don't have the dark hair and olive skin that marks our family. I have strawberry-blonde hair and freckles. But he's always been fond of Honor. If he is willing to sacrifice her to assure our position, he must really have been worried about a takeover.

"What can Byron even do for him?" I ask, half angry, half wondering.

Honor lifts one shoulder. "He has everyone intimidated. Judges. Drug suppliers. He's working both sides."

I stare at the place where the bruises are. I can't see them when the fabric rests naturally away from her skin. I'm sure that's on purpose. She must keep an inventory of where her bruises are and make sure they're covered up. It makes me exhausted—and desperate.

"Then let's go," I say. We don't need Gio to take us away. We can leave ourselves.

She frowns, her delicate eyebrows drawing together. "What are you saying?"

"I'm saying let's run away. Just you and me." My throat goes tight as I imagine never seeing Gio again. And I tell her the same thing I told him, though my voice cracks this time. "It will be an adventure."

Her head is shaking *no no no.* "They'd find us. There's no way, Clara. Don't even say the words."

But I've already said them. And once they're out, I can't put them away. Not when I close my eyes and see the dark bluish imprint of Byron's fingers. "We'll find some way to hide. To go underground. It has to be better than this, than you getting hurt."

"And what will we do for money?"

"I don't know. Something. I don't need all this." I wave my hand to indicate the ornate antique furniture and expensive artwork. These aren't things I chose for myself. They are part of the cage that keeps me here. Money and family and obligation. All of them bind me.

"It's impossible," she says, her voice wistful. "I thought of leaving once. I even had a plan. But…"

"But what?"

"But you're still a minor, Clara. You couldn't work. You couldn't even be seen."

My heart clenches. I would be a liability to her. "You could leave without me."

Her eyes flare with something—memory? Betrayal? Our mother left us both. The official story is that she died in a car crash. But everyone knows she wasn't allowed to drive. And the casket at her funeral was closed. If she did drive that day, she was leaving. And if she died that day, it means my father caught her.

"I will never leave you." She says it like a vow— fierce.

My eyes grow hot with tears. "Me either," I promise her. Even if Gio showed up, ready to take me away. Even if that girlish dream came true. I'd never leave without Honor. She's my sister. I love her. And that's why I can't stand by and let Byron hurt her. There's no fighting a man like that.

The only way to keep her safe is to take her away.

✧   ✧   ✧

THE NEXT NIGHT I creep across the grass. The bottoms of my feet feel extra sensitive when I do this. Maybe my sense of touch is heightened because of fear. Or because I'm about to see Gio. I can feel every blade of grass tickle my feet, every bump and dip in the earth. Even the night air becomes a tactile thing, blowing gently against my skin, leaving goose bumps in its wake.

When I reach the pool house, the door opens. "Clara," he whispers.

I smile back, relieved. A part of me had worried that he wouldn't come tonight. He'd seemed freaked out by the kiss. All through eating samples of pork forestiere and shrimp kabobs from the caterer, I'd been thinking about him. What was he eating? What was he thinking?

The pool house is dark, like always.

I slip inside and toss myself on the couch, like always.

He looks outside to make sure no one spotted me. Like always.

Then he shuts the door and makes his way over to me. This is different, though. He's walking stiffly. Strangely. It stirs a memory in me. The way Honor sometimes walks when Byron has been rough with her.

I sit up. "Are you hurt?"

He doesn't answer. He just sits down—slowly. Carefully.

"You *are* hurt," I say, accusing. Then I'm up and by his side, hands hovering. I don't want to touch whatever bruise he has and make it worse. "What happened?"

"It's nothing."

I shut my eyes. The only two people in my life I care about are being beaten, being abused, and I am helpless to stop it. "Your father?"

"Not this time."

I kneel beside the armchair he's in. "Who then?"

He sighs and leans his head all the way back. "Some assholes."

I run my hands over his leg that's closest to me—his thigh, his calf, his ankles. He doesn't flinch or pull away, so I hope that means this side is okay. "Where does it hurt? I can get some ice."

"No ice." His voice has gone deeper.

A part of me, some deep and ancient part of me, knows it's because my hands are on him. It makes me bolder. I move closer, between his legs now. "Or maybe some bandages? Did you have any cuts? You should put antibiotics in them so you don't get an infection."

His laugh is harsh. "No bandages, *bella*."

God, his voice when he says that. I can almost forget he's injured. I can almost forget he's seventeen and I'm fifteen. I can forget that our fathers would kill us if they found us together.

"What then?" If I can make him feel better a different way, I will. I run my hands up his calves, his thighs—his hands grab my wrists, stopping me.

"No anything," he says, his voice thick with pain. Or with something else.

I don't fight his hold on my wrists. I let him keep me there. And I rest my head on his thigh. It's not really meant to be seductive, even though I can feel the slope of his jeans. Even though I can see the bulge just inches away from my face. I know he's not going to do anything dirty to me. I'd probably like it if he did, but he won't. Just like he won't kiss me again. But he doesn't make me move away.

Instead he lets out an unsteady breath and releases my wrists. I remain there, kneeling in front of him, resting my cheek on his thigh.

His broad hand brushes over my temple, my cheek. He plays with the braid of my hair for a moment before resuming his gentle, rhythmic stroking. He's not touching anywhere below my neck, but my whole body lights up with it, tense and languorous at the same time.

It's a strange feeling, like being a beloved pet. An owned thing. Cared for. Cherished.

It's somehow sweeter than being the unwanted bastard daughter.

"I shouldn't let you come here," he mutters.

"Don't," I say. I can't bear when he talks like that, as if he might not show up one of these days. It's a lifeline for me, a breath of air while I'm drowning. And if I run away with Honor, then each one of these visits could be my last. Tears spring to my eyes, dampening the denim of his jeans.

"Shh," he soothes. "I won't make you stop."

He traces the line of my jaw and the curve of my ear. His blunt finger trails all the way down my neck.

"So pretty," he says. "Do you know, *bella?* I hurt with it, how pretty you are."

And then I'm hurting too, his words like whiskey.

They will take getting used to. I need so much more.

"Byron is hurting her," I whisper. Because it's the only way I know how to tell him. *We'll have to leave soon. I can't let him keep hurting her.*

His hand stills, and I think he must understand my secret message. "All the men hurt women here," he says. His tone is so dark, so unlike him.

I look up at him. "Gio?"

His hand encircles my neck, forcing my chin up. He just rests his hand there, his palm flush against my skin. Not squeezing. Just holding. "Are you afraid of me?"

I tremble because of the pain in his expression, in his voice. I am afraid—for my sister, for him. I'm afraid I'll break down and stay just so I can be near him, even if that means condemning my sister for life. But I'm not afraid that he'll hurt me. "No."

"You should be." He leans forward and whispers in my ear. "I've done things you couldn't imagine."

A tear slides down my cheek. Whatever these things are, they cause him pain. I see it in him. I feel it. And he has no choice—no more than Honor has a choice.

"You'd never hurt me," I say. My voice is wobbling because I'm hurting for him. But I mean every word. It's not the first time he's tried to scare me away. I'm not afraid of him.

The anger I feel in him slides away, replaced by something else. Desire.

His eyes are almost glowing in the moonlight streaming through the window. He removes his hand from my neck. His thumb brushes over my lips, back and forth. Back and forth.

My breath catches. Without even thinking, my lips part.

Then the tip of his thumb is pressing inside my mouth. He gently nudges my lips further apart. I don't understand all that's happening, don't know everything he wants, but I know how to take his lead. This is just like kissing, except instead of his lips and his tongue, it's his thumb.

He presses until his thumb is half in my mouth, and then it's only natural to close my lips and suck gently. He makes a soft sound, like a grunt. It sounds like need. Like relief.

The texture of his thumb is rough on my tongue. I slide it against him. He makes a hissing sound and shifts his hips. I never realized my tongue has this much power. Just a flick and the large frame of him tightens.

Before I am ready, he removes his thumb. It's still wet from my mouth when he rubs it along my lips, painting them, at first hot and then cold when he pulls away completely.

I feel like I'm in a trance when I stare up at him. He could ask me for anything, and I'd give it.

He knows that.

He leans forward and places a chaste kiss on my forehead. "Tomorrow," he says. "I'll see you tomorrow."

CHAPTER THREE

I STARE AT the wood paneling, holding my breath. I'm not sure what I think this is going to accomplish. Still, I can't quite bring myself to knock. My father is waiting on the other side of that door.

Did he notice the cigars I took?

I'd be in trouble then. But even more trouble if he found out I've been sneaking out of the house.

My palms are damp, my breathing erratic. Once I knock on the door, I'll hear my father's voice. *Come in.* He answers that way every time. He's said those words to me more often than my own name. The sound of him saying them is both comforting and scary.

When I got the summons to come downstairs, I considered going to my sister. I needed her to give me a hug and tell me everything is going to be all right. But she has her own problems to deal with, including a puffy eye and split lip.

And I'm old enough now to know those promises are empty.

She can't make sure this turns out all right. Not for me and not for herself.

I take a deep breath and blow it out. Then I knock.

"Come in."

Shock races down my spine. I can't make myself move. I know exactly whose voice that is. Not my father's.

The door opens in front of me. It's not sweet, like when Giovanni does it. Not chivalrous. Byron looks impatient. "I said come in," he snaps.

I jump, imagining that voice snapping at Honor, those hands hurting her. He doesn't wait to see if I follow him—he already knows that I will. And I do, shutting the door behind me, a hollow feeling in my stomach. I regret not going to see my sister now, even though it wouldn't have helped. In fact she might have insisted on coming with me as a show of support, and that would just get her hurt even more.

If anyone's getting hurt now, it will be me.

"Sit down," Byron says more calmly, perching on the edge of the desk.

My father sits in his chair, watching me with a blank expression. Why didn't he tell me to come in? Because he's just a figurehead now. He knows it. I know it.

And Byron sure as heck knows it.

My father leans forward. "I've been talking to Byron about your work. I showed him some of your paintings."

My eyebrows shoot up. I thought he barely knew about my painting. And to think he showed them to someone else, like a proud father? My throat gets tight.

"It's important for young girls to have hobbies," Byron says. "I've been trying to get Honor to pick up riding, but she claims she's afraid of horses."

My eyes narrow, but I force them to look normal. Honor doesn't *claim* she's afraid of horses—she *is* afraid of them. And maybe if she wasn't busy dodging his fists and doctoring herself, she'd have more time for hobbies.

As if Byron senses my anger, he smiles. "But you are different from her, aren't you?"

Is that a jab at my parentage? I snap my gaze to my father. Something dark flickers in his eyes. And that's it. There was a time a man could be beaten for even implying dishonor. And here was this man, with his shiny shoes and his slick hair and his *butt* on my father's desk, getting away with everything.

It makes me angry. "Is there a reason you called me, Papa?"

"Byron and I would like you to attend the party."

Sweet. Finally I get to be part of something. And hey, it's my sister's engagement party. Even if she is getting engaged to a monster, I should be there.

Just as quickly, suspicion rolls through me. "Just last week you were saying I'm too young. Why did you change your mind?"

My father's hard expression slips, and just for a moment I see the desperation underneath. He's a man holding on to the ledge. And one of these days, he's going to get a push—from the man sitting on his desk.

Byron's genial expression doesn't fool me for a second. "I convinced him you were a big girl," he says with a wink. "You are, aren't you?"

What a creep. "Of course I am."

The look he gives my body then is bold and disgusting. His gaze settles on my breasts, and *big girl* takes on a totally different meaning. The corner of his mouth lifts in a slight sneer. I feel like I could shower for days and never get clean.

"Can I go now?" I ask, keeping my voice as even as possible. "I have to figure out a dress if I'm going to the party tomorrow night."

"Of course," my father says, waving me off.

"Oh, and Clara." Byron fingers a pen in a way that somehow looks menacing. "Be sure to look your best. There are some friends of mine I'm having you meet."

I WASN'T EXAGGERATING about the dress. Having spent most of my life cooped up in my bedroom or the library, I don't have the kind of fancy dresses everyone will be wearing tonight.

"You can wear one of mine," Honor says when I tell her the good news. Well, *somewhat* good news. The prospect of going to the party seemed less exciting after that creepy look from Byron. And his mention of friends. I have no desire to meet anyone he'd call a friend.

Still, I can't deny that I'm excited. My first party.

"There's no way that's going to work," I tell her honestly.

Honor is slender. And I'm...not. I'm five years younger than Honor, but somehow my bust is actually bigger. So are my hips.

She rolls her eyes and still manages to look classy and mature while she does it. "We'll make a few alterations if we have to."

"*If* we have to? Oh, we'll have to. And by alterations, I'm guessing you mean adding an entire extra dress. Like if we tie two together, there might be enough fabric."

Her lips twist disapprovingly. "We aren't that different, Clara."

Yeah, right. We're different in every way. Her black hair to my pale. Her smooth olive skin to my pink freckled skin. Her slim body to my full one. "Have you looked in a mirror lately? You're beautiful."

"What are you talking about? Clara, you're gorgeous. There are women who'd love to have your curves. And your pretty hair."

I just stare at her. I don't believe her at all.

She sighs. She must know I'm a lost cause. "You have no idea how adorable your freckles are, do you?"

"Just what every girl wants to be. Adorable. You look like Audrey Hepburn come to life."

That makes her laugh. "Wouldn't that be nice. I could go off on a holiday in Rome."

"You'd have to escape first," I remind her. That's how the movie goes. We've both watched it a hundred times. There's only so many things you can do while stuck in a mansion. Read a book. Practice yoga with a DVD instructor.

"Well," she says lightly. "That can be for later. For

now, we need to get you dressed. And I have an idea."

She digs through her closet and comes up with a black wrap dress. The fabric has enough give that I can fit into it. It expands to accommodate my hips, falling above my knees instead of below, looking flirty instead of vintage. It's cute.

I stare at myself in the mirror. Really cute.

Except…

"That's not going to cut it," Honor says, staring at my cleavage. It's hard not to stare. My cleavage is practically busting out of this dress, straining at the top.

So much for looking my best. "I'm hopeless."

She shakes her head. "Nothing a little double-sided tape can't solve. We'll add a shawl that covers up the rest."

She disappears to find this magical tape and shawl that's going to fix me. With her gone, I suck in my stomach and lift my body, in what I guess is a seductive pose. The truth is I have no idea what seduction would be like. My mind flashes to Giovanni's hand stroking my hair, my neck. His thumb brushing my lips. And then slipping between them, resting on my tongue.

My whole body flushes warm.

I imagine Giovanni in the room with me. What would he think of this dress?

What would he think of this cleavage? I wonder if I'll get a chance to show him. He might be at the party. My mind is awash in fantasies. Dancing on the ballroom floor. Stealing a kiss in the garden.

I know they're stupid dreams. His father is a foot soldier—they don't often get invited to these kinds of affairs, much less their underage sons. And even if Gio came, would he dance with me? Or would that tip off our fathers that we knew each other?

There are a hundred reasons why it's a bad idea. But sometimes it feels like if I want it enough, if I wish hard enough, it might happen anyway.

WE ARE LOUNGING side-by-side on the old, musty sofa. One earbud is in my left ear, the other is in Gio's right. Above us, dust floats in the moonlight. I'm back in my standard jeans and tank top. No longer glamorous or over-the-top sexy. But this moment feels so perfect it almost hurts. I want a million of these moments, strung like beads on a necklace, one after the other.

When the third *Glee* song comes on, Giovanni slants me a dark look that makes me giggle.

"What?" I ask, going for innocent. But I don't quite succeed. I like making him suffer with fun songs. He doesn't tell me that much about his life outside of these nights, but I know there's not enough fun in it.

"Really?" he says.

I sing along. "*Don't stop believing...*"

He groans, but I see the smile that plays on his lips. He likes it. "You know high school is nothing like that show, right?"

"Duh," I say. "That's not even realistic. It's obviously

27

more like *Buffy the Vampire Slayer*."

He flicks his thick fingers lightly against my arm. "Smart-ass."

I stick my tongue out, which probably proves him right. I don't care. "Hey, it's not my fault I never got to go. If it were up to me, I wouldn't have to guess what high school is like. I would already know."

"I don't agree with much your father does, but I think he got that part right."

Stung, I face the ceiling again. "Whatever."

"I'm just saying people would know who your father is. It makes you a target."

"So I should just never live, is that what you're saying? I should just stay locked up and marry whoever he tells me to and dress however Byron says—"

"What the fuck are you talking about? What did Byron tell you?" He's facing me, eyes a little wild.

Unease rolls through me. Gio and I, we've had our little spats. It's part of the teasing ups and downs we do. But I've never seen him quite so intense. Except maybe about his father. But then he mostly shuts down if that topic comes up.

He's not shutting down now. His expression is furious and expectant.

"He didn't tell me anything," I say, trying to calm him down. "He just said I was going to the party. And that I should look my best, whatever that means."

Gio swears in Italian. I mostly don't understand the words except to know they're bad.

"That fucker," he says.

Okay, I know that one. "It's not a big deal."

"It's a big fucking deal. He needs to keep his filthy fucking hands off you—"

"He didn't touch me." I prop myself up on one elbow, concerned. Cautiously, like approaching a wild animal, I rest my hand on Gio's arm. "He didn't touch me, okay?"

I watch Gio take deep breaths in and out. He calms down slowly, though I sense the rage is still simmering beneath the surface. After a beat, I lie back down. The song changes to *Angels We Have Heard on High*. It's early May, but I love Christmas music any time of year. It's so hopeful. I especially love the *Glee* version.

Maybe I did think high school was a little like that...

"I thought you weren't allowed to go to the party," he says, his voice low.

I shrug. "I guess they changed their mind."

"It's not safe for you."

Umm... "Everyone will be there."

"That's exactly why it's not safe."

"Will you be there?" I ask hopefully. I'm not worried about the safety of this party. I mean...it's a *party*. But I want him to be there anyway. "You could protect me."

He lets out a disgusted sound. "No. I have a job that night."

A job. That sounds ominous. It's not like he's got shifts at a movie theater or something. A job means something for his father. Something for *la familia*. What if something goes wrong? What if he gets hurt? He still has bruises from whatever awful thing happened the other night. How dare his father send him into violent, dangerous situations.

Then again, that's exactly what my father is doing with Honor.

"We'll see each other after," I say. I was thinking of telling him we'd skip that night, but lying here with him now, that feels too painful. And now that I know he has a job, I'd just be worried about him until I saw him again.

"The party will be late."

"I'll leave early. I'll tell them I feel sick or something." I don't mention that I already feel sick. I've wanted to go to a party, to *anything,* since forever. But now that it's here, it feels all wrong. This isn't about dancing in ballrooms and getting kissed in the garden. This is being paraded in front of Byron's friends while Gio is off somewhere risking his life. "Please. I need to see you after the party. Meet me here."

He grunts, still looking at the ceiling. "Maybe."

CHAPTER FOUR

THE PARTY IS a success. I know this because at least five people have told me so. How good the food is. How pretty the flowers are. How grown up I look in this dress. It makes me wonder if they want something from me.

Of course they want something from me.

Maybe I'm just being cynical. The people do seem very nice...if a little superficial. Every conversation I've had has been about the weather and the best wine vintage. And the weather again.

I miss lounging on the couch, choking down whiskey or listening to music. I miss resting my head on Gio's strong thigh, feeling the warm weight of his hand on the back of my neck.

I miss him.

"Dear?"

My attention snaps back to the woman in front of me. It's almost hard to see her face with all the diamonds crowding her neck and earlobes. "I'm sorry, Mrs. Donato. I didn't hear you."

It helps that the ballroom is crazy loud. It makes it less weird that she has to keep repeating herself to me.

"Call me Ines," she says with a knowing smile. "You're practically a woman now. One of us."

One of us. But who is that exactly?

It's like there's a secret handshake that no one ever taught me. I understand what Gio meant about staying in the background and hoping not to be noticed. There's something almost creepy about all the smiles and the wealth. And the congratulations for my sister, when everyone here knows what a monster Byron is.

Heck, everyone here *is* a monster.

All the jewels dripping from wrists and necks were bought with blood. But I'm supposed to smile and say, "I'm so thrilled to be here."

She clucks. "It's so hot though. More than usual, don't you think?"

"Yes, it has been warm this year."

Which is a lie. We live in Las Vegas. It's basically a giant oven, a kiln that's been baking the cracked clay earth for centuries. The grounds of my father's estate are lush green, a testament to what huge sums of money and half the city's water supply can accomplish.

We've made our own little oasis. But that doesn't make it any less of an illusion.

I scan the crowd, but I'm too short to see above the black tuxes and fancy hairdos. "Have you happened to see Honor around?"

Mrs. Di Donato winks. "I saw her leaving the ballroom with Byron a few minutes ago. Young love is a beautiful thing."

I manage some kind of nod that convinces her before making my excuses. Then I'm crossing the ballroom. I readjust the shawl as I go, making sure it's covering my cleavage. My feet are aching after hours of standing in heels—seriously, whoever invented these was a masochist. Or a sadist. But they don't slow me down. Whatever is going on between Honor and Byron, it's not love. I have to check on her.

A man stops in front of me. I start to go around him, but he touches my arm.

I flinch back. Only then do I realize he was stopping me on purpose.

He smiles. "Are you Clara?"

I've never seen this man before. And I have no desire to meet him now. "Excuse me. I'm looking for my sister."

He grins, mouth stretching wide. He looks kind of like a movie star, and I don't like it. "I'm afraid she's indisposed at the moment. I hope that will give you a few minutes to talk to me."

I'm standing in the middle of hundreds of people, but I've never felt more alone. I don't know where Honor is. She could be anywhere in the house. Heck, she could have left the house. And with Byron, who is no doubt hurting her in some way. He will always hurt her. There's no way we can stop him. As I stand in the crowded room, a deep and sorrowful certainty takes root.

We have to go. Leave. There's no reason to wait.

There's no reason to hope things will get better.

The only thing to do is leave—and never see Gio again.

"Excuse me," I say again, this time more quietly. I'm breaking apart inside. "I think I need to be alone."

His expression turns apologetic. "Actually, Honor sent me to check on you. She knew she'd be busy and wanted to make sure you had someone by your side."

I narrow my eyes. Is he flat out lying to me? It feels that way. Honor would know I don't want some weirdo stranger hovering around me. But then again, she does get protective sometimes. Maybe she did worry about me in the ballroom by myself.

But why not send someone I actually knew? Or at least introduce me to him first?

Then again, it's not like Byron would have given her time to do anything. If he says to jump off a cliff, he's already pushing you off. That's how he operates.

I look back at the party. I *do* feel sick now. Sick of smiling. Sick of pretending. I want to be in the pool house, teasing Giovanni. But it's still my sister's party. And I don't need to listen to my intuition to know she might be hurting right now. I have to find her before I go. I'll make sure she's okay. Then I'll make excuses so I can sneak to the pool house.

"Can you bring me to my sister?" I ask the strange man.

"Of course." His smile disarms me. He actually looks pretty nice when he's not blocking my path and being pushy. "She just stepped outside for some air."

✧   ✧   ✧

THE LIGHTS STRUNG up over the patio cast the rest of the lawn into darkness. I can't even see the outline of the pool house from here. A couple is making out, half-hidden by a bush, but they stop when they see us. Actually, not us. Him. Whoever this guy is, he makes their eyes widen and they run inside, straightening their clothes as they go.

"Where's my sister?" I say.

He absently scans the dark landscape. "She'll be along."

It's not only secluded here. It's quiet. Much quieter than the voices and five-string orchestra inside. It makes me feel a little stranded, being out here alone with him, with no one to hear me. "Umm, what did you say your name was again?"

"Markam," he says with an easy smile. "Javier Markum."

My eyebrows shoot up. Wasn't he in the news about some big controversy? "The governor's son?"

"Does my reputation precede me?"

I can't remember what he'd supposedly done. But no one in that ballroom has clean hands. Not even me. We all benefit from the criminal enterprise in some way, even if it's only the bed we sleep in or the guards that lock us in. "Not really."

"Good." A glint enters his eyes. "I don't want us to get off on the wrong foot."

Suspicion is a dark knot in my chest. "Are you

friends with Byron?"

"Good friends, yes. We go way back."

My heart pounds. Honor would never send one of Byron's friends to me. She wouldn't trust him any more than I do. "He said something about wanting me to meet his friends. Was he talking about you?"

Dark eyes study me. "Direct. I like that in a girl. I hope we can speak frankly with each other."

"Why would that matter?"

"Because we're going to be seeing a lot more of each other. At least, if I have my way." He winks to lighten the words, but I can read between the lines. He always gets his way.

"I don't understand."

He shrugs. "You know how these things work. Powerful people make powerful enemies. We need to stick together. Like Byron and Honor, for example."

We are nothing like Byron and Honor. They're engaged. And if that was a marriage proposal, it was seriously lame. "I'm fifteen."

That earns me a chuckle. He has handsome features and an expensive tux, but he's twisting and distorting while I look at him. Everything looks exaggerated, fake. His smile. His hair. Even the good humor in his eyes. It's a creepy kind of humor. "I know you're too young for anything serious. We're just getting to know each other. Getting to know if…there'd even be a point in pursuing this, understand?"

No. "And if there is?"

"Then you'd still stay here, finish your studies. You'd be under Byron's protection. I'd visit from time to time."

In other words, he'd be free to play the field while I'd stay locked up in here. Gross. "I'd like to find my sister now."

"Look, Clara." He drops his head. It's an endearing move. A practiced move. "The truth is, Byron didn't only introduce me to you because of the family connections we could make. He thought I'd like you...and I do."

Somehow I don't think he's talking about my personality. "Why would he think that?"

"You have a certain innocence. A youthfulness I find appealing."

It's called being in high school, jackass. "Well, thanks. I guess. I'd like to find my sister, though. I'm worried about her."

"You never have to worry about her. Byron would never let anything happen to her."

That's what I'm afraid of. I take a step back. Then there's a hand clamped around my wrist. Javier's hand. "Let me go."

He pulls me closer. I wobble on my high heels, almost falling into him. The shawl comes lose. His gaze drops and darkens.

"Clara, I think you and I really get along."

"Let go of me *now.*"

He walks forward, and I have no choice but to walk backward, stumbling as I go. One of my shoes twists off, and then the other. I'm off balance, almost falling, except that he's holding me up, fingers clenched into my skin, wrenching me. The trellis is at my back, the same metal trellis I use to climb down, the one I use to escape, and now it's part of my prison. I'm caught between those unforgiving bars and his body, breath coming fast. Now I understand how Honor feels. I understand why she puts up with it—because she has no choice. I knew it before, but I never experienced it until now, never felt fear like a living thing inside me, clawing its way up my throat.

I kick at him, even as part of me knows that will only make it worse. I don't have the poise and class and core of steel that Honor has. I can't endure this, even when I know I have to. I can only fight.

"You little bitch," he snaps as my knee connects with his shin.

He twists my wrist, and I'm facing the wall. The scarf is long gone, and my breasts are pressing into the metal criss-cross. Javier is holding me in place, his breath hot against my temple. "I want us to get off on the right foot, Clara. I told you that."

And this is the right foot. Violence. Coercion. Tears stream down my face. There's no way out.

This is how Honor must feel. *Trapped.*

There is a sudden cry and groan from the man holding me captive, and then he's up against the metal grate himself, flat with arms spread wide, while Giovanni punches him again and again. The only reply Javier makes is a groaning sound that makes the hair rise up on my neck.

"Giovanni, stop!" He'll kill him, and that will be so much worse. He's the governor's son—and worse than that, he's Byron's friend. "Stop!"

Giovanni turns to see me, and the rage parts like dark clouds, long enough for me to see *him* looking back. Him, the boy who spent those nights in the pool house, cracking jokes and letting his hand brush against mine. The haze clears. "Clara?"

I'm crying, my hands clenched together as if in prayer. Begging. "Giovanni, please."

He turns and faces Javier. For a minute I think he's not going to listen. He's just going to keep beating him until Javier is dead, and then what will we do? I don't even know what we'll do if he's alive. We're in so much trouble. This goes beyond trouble.

Giovanni speaks low, so low I can barely hear him. "How does it feel without your buddies backing you up, huh? How does it feel one-on-one?"

Then he slams Javier into the wall one last time. Javier's eyes are closed as he slumps to the ground.

I stare at the unconscious man, his nose bloodied, his crisp tux rumpled and torn. "Is he...dead?"

Giovanni wipes his brow with his forearm. "No."

"Is he the one who did that to you? The bruises?" *With his buddies.*

"It doesn't matter."

"Yes, it does. Why would he—"

"We need to get out of here."

Right. What would happen if we were found out here? Every man in there is packing heat. Some of the women too. "We have to find Honor."

"There's not time." He puts his hand out to me. He doesn't grab me. Not like Javier did. His eyes are as dark as the night behind him—unfathomable. They scare me just as the night too, but I trust him. No matter how much he's tried to scare me away. No matter that he once stroked my neck, that he once held it in his hand.

I put my hand in his. "Let's go."

He doesn't wait. We run toward the pool house together. We don't even have to discuss it first. We both head toward there like it's our north star, our home.

I'm out of breath when we stumble inside. Adrenaline is like lava in my veins, making it too hot to stand still. Too hot to sit down. I can only pace in the small space, running my hair through my hands. "What are we going to do? Oh my God. *What are we going to do?*"

Gio takes my hands in his, and I finally stand still. I'm breathing hard, trembling.

"You have to go," he says. "It's not safe for you here anymore."

I know it's true. I knew it from the moment he first punched Javier, from the moment when Javier attacked me. I knew it even before then, when it was only Honor being hurt. But it's still hard to hear the words. This is my home, the only place I know. And for all that my father has been distant—and maybe not even truly related—he's the only parent I know.

"You're the one who told me my father was right to keep me here."

Gio swears in Italian. "He isn't fucking in charge anymore. You aren't safe here. You won't ever be safe here again."

I swallow hard. "Honor?"

"She'll go too. She won't fight it once she knows about Javier."

"And you, you'll come with us, right?"

He rests his forehead against mine. "Clara."

Panic rises in my chest. "Gio, you have to. He'll wake up. He'll tell them it was you."

CHAPTER FIVE

THE DOOR BURSTS open. I jump back from Giovanni, guilty and afraid of being caught touching—even though we have worse problems than that. It's not my father. Not even Byron. It's Honor.

Her gaze snaps to Giovanni, but she speaks to me. "Clara, I need a word with you. *Now.*"

She must have heard about Javier. I can tell by the strength of her voice—and the tremor hiding underneath. "You can say it in front of Gio," I tell her. "He already knows."

Honor's eyes narrow. She's wondering if we can trust him. She doesn't know him like I do.

"You have to get her out of here," Giovanni says. "There's not much time."

Slowly she shuts the door behind her and leans back against it. "I know."

"Take my car," he says. "It's gassed up. It should get you a few hundred miles. Then you'd better switch vehicles."

Honor nods. "That's better than the bus. I know they'll be checking."

Giovanni crosses the room and stands on the back of

the sofa. I can only stare as he reaches up to the vent that had been above us all those nights. He unhooks the grate and pulls out a black bag. "This has money," he says. "It's all I've got."

My sister takes it without question. "Thank you."

"Don't tell me where you're going," he says.

I can only stare at him. *Don't tell me where you're going.* As if he's not coming with us. As if he might get tortured for information. I grab Gio's arm. "What are you talking about? You need to come with us."

"Security," he says. "They're staying farther back from the house, but there's even more than usual around the gate."

"That means none of us can get out."

He shakes his head. "I'll cause a diversion. Distract them long enough so you can get out."

What? "No way."

"It's the only way."

I look at Honor. "This is crazy. Tell him he needs to come with us."

Her eyes are sad. Sadder than I've ever seen them. But also accepting. Of all people, she understands about sacrifice. "We don't have much time. The party is the best time to run, when they're distracted, when it will be hard for them to search the house. Especially if he can pull the guards away from the gate. We need to go now."

"No." I take a step back. "This can't be happening."

Gio looks at my sister. "Can you give us a minute?"

Her dark eyes study me. After a beat, she nods. "I'll

go scout the best path out of here."

"But the guards?" I tell her.

A ghost of a smile crosses her face. "I still have some friends here."

Then she's gone, leaving only Gio and me. Alone together. Just like we have been every night. Except totally different. Because this time tomorrow I'll be gone. And Gio will be…where? Here. Except if they find out he helped us, they'll hurt him.

And once Javier wakes up, they'll kill him.

"Gio, no."

He runs a hand down my arm—so lightly. His fingertips barely brush my skin. "Are you hurt?"

"I'm serious. We aren't doing this. I'm not kidding."

"I'm not joking." He sighs. "You don't know they'll take me. I'm not going to go easy."

"Yeah, but up against Byron? *Against all of them?*"

His gaze dips to my chest. "This dress, Clara."

The scarf is long gone, and all the running and freaking out have left my breasts almost popping out. I look like some kind of bombshell. I don't feel like a bombshell, though. I feel like a bomb that's about to go off if someone doesn't *listen* to me. The two people I love most are making plans about my life without me. Very serious plans that involve Gio getting hurt.

And I'm afraid nothing I say can stop them.

"You can't," I say, my voice soft and desperate.

"I just need a minute," he says, still staring at me in this dress.

"To what?"

"To remember this."

Fear grips my heart tighter than anything before. This can't be happening. I'd have let Javier touch me if I knew it would lead to this. I would let Javier do anything if it meant keeping Gio safe.

I can't stand him looking at me. Not because I don't want him to see. Because he's looking at me like a dying man would—as if he knows it's his last sight. As if drinking his fill.

My breath stutters. I need to be closer than this. This place we're in—this is water. And he is air. I push up to him, pull him down to me. I meet his lips in a gasp.

Then he's kissing me back, his lips demanding, tongue fierce. And his hands. Those large, beautiful hands that have done violence tonight—for me. They cradle my head so sweetly. How can something so good feel like pain? How can this be the end?

I shove him back. "We'll find another way. Something. Anything."

"There is no other way. This isn't the first time I've thought of how to get you out of here. And if you stayed here, you'd condemn your sister too. Byron would make everyone suffer."

And now it will only be Gio suffering. The canapés from the party turn in my stomach. My hands curl into fists, useless. "You wouldn't let me do this. You wouldn't let me sacrifice myself for you. So how can I let you?"

"You're not letting me do anything, Clara. You don't have a choice."

Angrily I shove the tears aside. This isn't a time to be sad, because this is *not* happening. We're not leaving him behind. So why can't I stop crying?

Why does it feel like I've already lost?

"Gio," I say, my voice breaking.

His forehead touches mine again, his hands cradling my face. I feel so delicate when he holds me like this. I feel loved. "Let me do this for you," he says roughly. "I couldn't protect you before. I don't have anything to offer. I never did. But this?"

"No, no," I sob.

He pushes me tighter against him, cheek to cheek, and I swear these tears aren't only mine. "You care too much, Clara."

"How is that too much? It's the right amount. I care too much to leave you here. How is that wrong?"

He is silent a moment. "It's not wrong. But I care too much to let you stay."

His arms come around me, holding me in. They feel unbreakable. They are castle walls, his arms. They are a drawbridge rolled up and a moat. They keep everyone out. Only with him do I feel completely safe. Maybe I'd always known how much he'd do for me. He'd fight for me. He'd die for me.

And that's what he's going to do. And at the end only rubble will be left.

"I'll be fine," he says, but we both know it's a lie.

My hands clench in his shirt. "How can you be?"

"Just go," he whispers fiercely. "You think this is about me sacrificing for you? No. I need you to do this for me, Clara. I need you to stay safe."

I cry until his shirt is dark and wet. These are silent tears. They fall without my consent, while my face is solemn. I can be stoic for him. I won't beg now. I won't plead.

Not even when Honor comes in and tells me it's time to go.

It feels like dying to walk away. Feels like dying to look back and see him watching me go. Feels like dying as I cross the dark lawn.

Honor holds my hand, but doesn't say anything.

I think she knows. It's the worst thing I've ever felt, to leave him behind. And it's nothing compared to what he'll go through.

We're near the gate when we hear the explosion behind us. *Fireworks.*

Those are the fireworks that would have celebrated her engagement.

Only fitting that they'll end it.

It's not hard to find Gio's beat-up Pontiac Grand Am parked down the side lane. The radio is broken. The gas tank is full. We drive in silence until the blasts fade to nothing.

There is only empty road in front of us and empty road behind.

I need you to do this for me, Clara. I need you to stay safe.

And so I do.

THE END

Thank you for reading the prequel to the Stripped series. Find out what happens to Honor and Clara while they are on the run. Turn the page for the first five chapters of Love the Way You Lie…

LOVE THE WAY YOU LIE

A dark romance about the lies that lead us down…

I'll do anything to get safe, even if that means working at the scariest club in town.

I'll do anything to stay hidden, even if it means taking off my clothes for strangers.

I'll do anything to be free. Except give him up. When he looks at me, I forget why I can't have him. He's beautiful and scarred. His body fits mine, filling the places where I'm hollow, rough where I am soft.

He's the one man who wants to help, but he has his own agenda. He has questions I can't answer. *What are you afraid of?*

You.

"I've always been a fan of Skye Warren ever since I read Wanderlust. Her writing is flawless and tales captivating. Love The Way You Lie is no exception. 5 Stars."

Pepper Winters,
New York Times bestselling author of Tears of Tess

CHAPTER ONE

I USED TO think there were things I'd never do. Never take my clothes off for money. Never sell my body. Never fuck a stranger just to survive. I'd never sink that low.

I'd rather die.

But it's hard to die, to lie down and let it happen. Not to fight. Not to reach toward the surface for air when you're drowning. It's almost impossible. I'm proof of that. I'm a living example of how low a person would go, if they have to. If they're desperate enough.

If they're staring at the black barrel of a gun, counting their breaths.

I hold my breath as I sweep red across my lips, stark against powder-pale skin. My eyes are already finished with heavy gold liner and shimmery shadow. A stranger blinks at me from the mirror, her eyes wide. She doesn't look sad. Or lonely. She doesn't look terrified, so the makeup's done its job.

On a Wednesday night, the changing room is empty. Even half-priced appetizers can't keep the club full in the middle of the week. No one would dance tonight unless they had to. That's why I'm here. Because I have to be.

Like Candy, who's onstage. And Lola, working the floor. We're doing what we have to do. We're counting our breaths.

I stand and shake out my wings, making sure they're still in place, attached to my bra. It only has to last until I strip it off. The song out there is getting louder and faster, and I know it'll be over soon. My turn next. *Lucky me.*

And I am lucky. I know exactly what the alternative is.

I smooth my panties into place, making sure they're covering the important parts. For now. *Panties* is a generous term for the scrap of fabric designed to tear apart when I tug.

I turn—and freeze. My breath leaves me in a whoosh. Blue is standing in the doorway, leaning against the frame. His thick arms bulge, stretching his T-shirt, tattoos covering the skin I can see. He's ex-military, but whatever sense of honor he might have had is long gone. He's still got discipline though. And power and *force*. He's the club's own mercenary.

How long has he been watching me?

I ignore the chill that slides down my spine. I ignore *him* as I walk toward the door. Maybe he'll move and let me pass. Maybe he won't harass me. And maybe pigs will fly. He grabs my arm.

Which is just as well. It's not like I could have gotten past him without shoving him or something. I'm a lot of things, but I'm not suicidal. So I stand there with his hand on my arm, feeling creepy-crawly tingles all up and down my skin. I don't look him in the eye. I don't like seeing the darkness there. Instead I stare past him, into the dark hallway.

"Not even going to say hi?" He smells like smoke and sweat and alcohol. At only eight o'clock in the evening.

I keep my voice steady. "Hi."

"That didn't sound very friendly. You got a problem with me? Did I offend you in some way?"

Jesus, I don't need this. The song's almost over. If I miss my cue... I shiver. I can't miss my cue. The hallway behind him is empty. Not that anyone would help if they saw. Ivan is the owner of the strip club, along with a cadre of other illegal shit in the city. He's gone most of the time, so even though Blue is just a bouncer, he gets free reign. At least he does a decent job of protecting us girls.

Even if he is an asshole.

"I don't have a problem with you," I say.

He pulls me closer until my body is almost flush with his—and still I won't look him in the eye. He doesn't pay for that. No one does. They pay to touch me, to hurt me. To fuck me. They don't pay me to look them in the eye, so I don't.

His mouth is close enough to my ear that I can feel the whiskers when he speaks. "Then why don't you prove it. Show me how friendly you can be."

Gross. "I'm up next."

His hold tightens, and I can already picture the

bruises. When I'm at home, in the shower, I'll wash off the stench of this place, the shame, but I won't be able to wash off the dark shape of his fingers where they press into my skin. He's imprinting himself on me, becoming part of me, and bile rises in my throat.

"I'm up next," I repeat in a whisper.

Even Blue doesn't want to anger the powers that be. I look up in time to see regret flicker in his eyes. He lets me go. "Later, Honey."

I flinch even though that's my name. Not my real name, but it's what they call me here.

It's who I am here.

When he steps aside, I hurry down the dark hallway. I'm almost more agile in heels than I am barefoot, from all the practice. There are lights on either side of the hallway, track lighting to make the walk feel glamorous or maybe to make sure we don't trip in our stilettos. It feels out of place in the strip club, lighting up what is better dark, dusty corners and ambient shame. It reminds me of a landing strip—not in stripper terminology, but a real airstrip for airplanes with lights on either side to guide me. At any moment I could take off. At any moment, I could be free.

I have to believe that. It's the only way to keep going.

And then I'm backstage, waiting. Trapped. The opposite of free.

I stand behind the curtains. Twenty years ago this area would be filled with stagehands and costume designers and performers waiting for their cue. But now there's just me, shivering in the draft from the air-conditioning as the final strains of music fade away.

Candy slips back, skin shining with sweat and glitter, smelling of booze and cherries. She's the prettiest girl here, except for the track marks on her arms. Except for the black eyes she has too often, ones she skillfully covers with makeup.

The opening notes of my song start playing.

"Depressing," she tells me as she straightens the straps of my bra.

She's never been a fan of my song selection. Apparently, blues is a downer.

"It has a good beat," I say even though she's right. Of course she is. She definitely earns the most of anyone here, and Lola earns more than me too. But if I can't dance classical, I'll at least pick something I want to hear.

She laughs. "A good beat? You still think this is about dancing."

I shake my head, but I'm smiling. She has that effect on people, with her slutty schoolgirl outfit and pigtails. With her bubblegum-pop songs that she strips to. *Branding,* she calls it.

"What's it about then?"

"About fucking, of course." Then she's gone down the hallway, heading toward the dressing room.

My smile falters as I stare after her. What's more depressing than fucking?

I manage to push through the curtain only one beat after my cue. Not that anyone here would notice. Like she said, it's about fucking. About being naked and for sale. Not about dancing. So I drop one foot in front of the other, making my hips pop with each step. A black satin bra. Panties made of black ribbon. It's dark and sexy—and obvious. That's fine with me. I'd rather be forgettable. *I wish I could forget.*

In the first moments onstage, I'm always blinded.

The bright lights, the smoke. The wall of sound that feels almost tangible, as if it's trying to keep me out, push me back, protect me from what's going to happen next. I'm used to the dancing and the catcalls and the reaching, grabbing hands—as much as I can be. But I'm never quite used to this moment, being blinded, feeling small.

I reach for the pole and find it, swinging my body around so the gauzy scrap of fabric flies up, giving the men near the stage a view of my ass. I still can't quite make anything out. There are dark spots in my vision.

The smile's not even a lie, not really. It's a prop, like the four-inch heels and the wings that snap as I drop them to the stage.

Broken.

A few people clap from the back.

Now all that's left is the thin satin fabric. I grip the pole and head into my routine, wrapping around, sliding off, and starting all over again. I lose myself in the physicality of it, going into the zone as if I were running a marathon. This is the best part, reveling in the burn of my muscles, the slide of the metal pole against my skin and the cold, angry rhythm of the song. It's not like ballet, but it's still a routine. Something solid, when very few things in my life are solid.

I finish on the pole and begin to work the stage, moving around so I can collect tips. I can see again, just barely, making out shadowy silhouettes in the chairs.

Not many.

There's a regular on one side. I recognize him. Charlie. He tosses a five-dollar bill on the stage, and I bend down long and slow to pick it up. He gets a wink and a shimmy for his donation. As I'm straightening, I spot another man on the other side of the stage.

His posture is slouched, one leg kicked out, the other under his chair, but somehow I can tell he isn't really relaxed. There's tension in the long lines of his body. There's *power*.

And that makes me nervous.

I spin away and shake my shit for the opposite side of the room, even though there's barely anyone there. It's only a matter of time before I need to face him again. But I don't need to look at him. *They don't pay me to look them in the eye.*

Still I can't help but notice his leather boots and padded jacket. Did he ride a motorcycle? It seems like that kind of leather, the tough kind. Meant to withstand weather. Meant to protect the body from impact.

The song's coming to a close, my routine is coming to an end and I'm glad about that. Something about this guy is throwing me off. Nothing noticeable. My feet and hands and knowing smile still land everywhere they need to. Muscle memory and all that. But I don't like the way he watches me.

There's patience in the way he watches me. And patience implies waiting.

It implies planning.

I reach back and unclasp my bra. I use one hand to cover my breasts while I toss the bra to the back of the stage. I pretend to be shy for a few seconds, and suddenly I feel shy too. Like I'm doing more than showing my breasts to strangers. I'm showing *him*. And as I stand there, hand cupping my breasts, breath coming fast, I feel his patience like a hot flame.

This time I do miss the beat. I let go on the next one, though, and my breasts are free, bared to the smoky air and the hungry eyes. There are a few whistles from around the room. Charlie holds up another five-dollar bill. I sway over to him and cock my hip, letting him shove the bill into my thong, feeling his hot, damp breath against my breast. He gets close but doesn't touch. That's Charlie. He tips and follows the rules, the best kind of customer.

I don't even glance at the other side of the room. If the new guy is holding up a tip, I don't even care. He doesn't seem like the kind of guy who follows rules. I don't know why I'm even thinking about him or letting him affect me. Maybe my run-in with Blue made me more skittish than I'd realized.

All I have left is my finale on the pole. I can get

through this.

This part isn't as physically strenuous as before. Or as long. All I really need to do is grind up against the pole, front and back, emphasizing my newly naked breasts, pretending to fuck.

That's what I'm doing when I feel it. Feel *him.*

I'm a practical girl. I have to be. But there's a feeling I get, a prickle on the back of my neck, a churning in my gut, a warning bell in my head when I'm near one of *them.* Near a cop. My eyes scan the back of the room, but all I can see are shadows. Is there a cop waiting to bust someone? A raid about to go down?

My gaze lands on the guy near the stage. Him? He doesn't look like a cop. He doesn't *feel* like a cop. But I don't trust looks or feelings. All I can trust is the alarm blaring in my head: *get out, get out, get out.*

I can barely suck in enough air. There's only smoke and rising panic. Blood races through me, speeding up my movements. *A cop.* I feel it like some kind of sixth sense.

Maybe he feels my intuition about him, because he leans forward in his seat.

In one heart-stopping moment, my eyes meet his. I can see his face then, drawn from charcoal shadows.

Beautiful, his lips say. All I can hear is the song.

I'm not even on beat anymore, and it doesn't matter. It doesn't matter because there's a cop here and I have to get out. Even if my intuition is wrong, it's better to get out. Safer.

I'll never be safe.

The last note calls for a curtsy—a sexy, mocking movement I choreographed into my routine. Like the one I'd do at the end of a ballet recital but made vulgar. I barely manage it this time, a rough jerk of my head and shoulders. Then I'm gone, off the stage, running down the hallway. I'm supposed to work the floor next, see who wants a lap dance or another drink, but I can't do that. I head for the dressing room and throw on a T-shirt and sweatpants. I'll tell them I feel sick and have to leave early. They won't be happy and I'll probably have to pay for it with my tips, but they won't want me throwing up on the customers either.

I run for the door and almost slam into Blue.

He's standing in the hallway again. Not slouching this time. There's a new alertness to his stare. And something else—amusement.

"Going somewhere?" he asks.

"I have to… My stomach hurts. I feel sick." I step close, praying he'll move aside.

He reaches up to trace my cheek. "Aww, should I call the doctor?" His hand clamps down on my shoulder. "I wouldn't want anything bad to happen to you."

I grip my bag tight to my chest, trying to ignore the threat in his words. And the threat in his grip. I really *do* feel sick now, but throwing up on him is definitely not going to help the situation. "Please, I need to leave. It's serious. I'll make it up later."

He'll know what I'm saying. That I'll make it up to

him personally. I'm just desperate enough to promise that. Desperate enough to promise him anything. And he's harassed me long enough that I know it's a decent prize. I'm sure he'll make it extra humiliating, but I'm desperate enough for that too.

"Please let me go." The words come out pained, my voice thin. It feels a little like my body is collapsing in on itself, steel beams bending together, something crushing me from the outside.

Regret flashes over his face, whether for refusing my offer or forcing me that low. But this time he doesn't let me go. "There's a customer asking for you. He wants a dance."

CHAPTER TWO

THE GRAND USED to be a theater, back when the city did more tourist trade than drug trafficking. Back when you could walk down this street without getting mugged. They held ballets and operas and one infamous magic show where a man was killed by a faulty fake gun. Over the years the shows visited less and less. This whole part of the city became gutted, empty. Attempts to revitalize the theater failed because the good, rich folk who had money to spend on theater tickets didn't want to come to these streets.

Now the building is just a husk of its former glory— faded metallic wallpaper and ornate molding with the gold paint scraping off. Tables and chairs fill the smoky, dark floor. There is a balcony in the back, but it isn't open to the public.

The rooms for private dances used to be ticket stalls in what would have been the lobby.

They don't have doors. They barely even have walls. The front window partitions have been ripped away, with only brass rods and velvet curtains to cover them.

The first is occupied by Lola. A flash of red fabric and a long mane of hair between the curtain tells me that much. And I know from her position on the floor and the soft groans that he's paid for more than a dance.

The second room is empty.

The third room is the farthest from the main floor. The darkest. I can only make out a shadow seated in the chair. All I want is to get the hell out of here, but Blue is standing behind me, crowding me, and the only way to get space, the only place to go is inside.

I slip past the heavy velvet curtain and wait for my eyes to adjust. Even before they do, I know it will be him. Not safe, rule-following Charlie. It's the other man. The new one. The one with the strange intensity in his stare.

I see the outline of his jacket first. And his boots, forming that same configuration—one leg shoved out, one under the chair. That's the way he sits, almost sprawled on the uncomfortable wooden chair. He's watching me. Of course he's watching me. That's what he paid to do.

"What'll it be?" I ask.

"What's on the menu?" he counters, and I know what he means. He means extra services. The same thing that Lola is doing now. More than just a dance. He looks out from the shadows like the Cheshire cat, all eyes and teeth and challenge. All he's missing are purple stripes filling in.

And if he's a cop, he can bust me just for offering it. Cops should have better things to do with their time. But I already know cops don't do what they should. I know that too well.

I'm running from one.

"A dance, of course." I run through the prices for fifteen minutes, thirty minutes. No one needs longer than that. They either go to the bathroom to jerk off or come in their pants.

"And if I want more than that?"

Now that my eyes have adjusted, now that I'm up close, I can see the tats at the base of his neck and on his wrists. They are probably along his arms and maybe his chest. There's ink on his hands too, though I can't make out what it says.

His black shirt is tight enough to show me his shape, the broad chest and flat abs. Underneath the shirt is a chain or necklace. I can only see the imprint, but it makes me want to pull up the fabric and find out what it is.

He wears his leathers like a second skin, like they're armor and he's a fighter. I can't really imagine him walking through a precinct in a blue shirt. He's not a cop. But there was that feeling, when I was onstage. I *felt* his interest, more than sexual. I felt his suspicion. I felt every instinct telling me he is there for more than a dance. I can't afford not to listen.

"There's no more than that," I answer flatly.

He grunts, clearly displeased. But it doesn't sound like he's going to force the issue—or complain to Blue. "Then dance."

Right. That's why I'm here. That's not disappointment, heavy in my gut. I don't expect anything from men except to get paid. So I dance, starting slow, moving my hips, my arms, touching my breasts. I'm a million miles away like this. I'm lying on my back, feeling crisp grass underneath my legs, looking up at the night sky.

It almost works, except that I need to get close to him. I need to climb onto him, straddling his legs with mine, reaching for the back of the chair to shake my tits in his face. And when I do, I smell him. He smells…not like smoke. Not like sweat.

He smells like my daydream, like grass and earth and clean air.

I freeze above him, body crouched, my breasts still shivering with leftover momentum.

"Something wrong?" he asks.

And his voice. God, his voice. It's gone rough and low, all the way to the ground. It slides along the creaky wood of the chair and the concrete floor and vibrates up my legs. It shimmers through the air and brushes over my skin, that voice. We're not touching in any place, but I can feel him just the same.

I swallow hard. "Nothing's wrong, sugar."

"Then sit down."

He means on his lap. Touching. It's against the rules, officially.

Unofficially it's one of the tamer things that happen in this room. "What if I don't want to?"

One large shoulder lifts, making the leather sigh. "I won't make you."

I hear the unspoken word *yet* ring in the air.

I should probably refuse him. Whether he's a cop or not, he's throwing me off. That's dangerous. And if there's some other cop in the building? That's even more dangerous.

But for some reason, I lower myself until I'm resting on his jeans, my posture awkward and off balance—until he shifts, and suddenly I'm sliding toward him, flush against him while I straddle his legs. Then his arms circle my body, trapping me. Any second now he's going to grope me. Maybe take his dick out and fuck me like this. It wouldn't be the first time.

But he just stays like that, arms firm but gentle. A hug. This is a hug.

Jesus. How long has it been since a man hugged me? Just that, without touching anywhere else, without his dick inside me? A long time.

My throat feels tight. "What next?" I ask again, and this time I'll offer anything on the menu. The real menu, with sex and pain and whatever else he's into.

"I'd like to touch you," he says, his breath brushing against my temple.

I know that's not all. We haven't even negotiated a price, but I find myself agreeing, silent and still.

I look into his eyes and feel something—familiarity. Do I know him from somewhere?

A hundred men come through here. They are nothing to me, and yet I can't help thinking I would remember him if he had come in another night. I can't shake the feeling I've seen him before. Met him. *Known him.*

I should be afraid. And I am, but I'm also wondering about the tattoo on the back of his hand. What does it mean? Then I have other things to wonder about, because that hand is touching me.

He doesn't start with my breasts or even my ass. Not the obvious places, the important ones. He starts with one hand at the back of my neck. My heart pounds heavy in my chest, almost bursting free. I can't get enough air. And suddenly this seems like an important place after all, so vulnerable. So small within the careful hold of his hand. How is it possible that his hands are so large?

He slides his other hand under my chin, lifting my face. And looks me in the eye. I can't look away. His eyes are dark and bottomless, the light glinting like distant stars.

"What's your name?" he mutters.

Honor. I almost say it, but that's not who I am here. Besides, they announced me when I went onstage. He doesn't seem like the type to forget, not when he asked for me after, not with his hands cradling my head, careful with me but faintly threatening. Because he could snap my neck in a second. He knows it. I know it. I even think Blue waiting outside knows it, but it all comes down to trust.

And I don't trust him.

"Honey," I whisper.

He repeats my name like he's never heard of it before. "Honey."

My gaze drops to his mouth, which is firm and almost thin. A hard man's lips, with scruff shadowing his jaw. "And yours?"

Those lips curve into a half smile. "You're better off not knowing my name."

That much I believe. It makes me trust him more. "I'm better off not sitting on your lap. Better off not taking my clothes off for strange men every night. I guess that ship has sailed."

His lids lower with something like appreciation. "You can call me Kip." He must have seen I didn't quite believe him, because he laughs softly. "It's my real name. Not like Honey."

I wince at the pointed jab, but what does he expect? The truth?

There is no truth. Honey isn't my real name, but as each day goes by, I feel less and less like Honor Moretti. I'm transparent, like a ghost. Insubstantial. That's what hiding does to you. It makes you invisible.

He relents at whatever expression's on my face, softening. "It's short for Kipling."

Just those few words and he's given me something. Something personal. Something real. That's rare in this club. That's rare in the whole world. It makes me want more. I've seen the jut of old bone from the ground. I want to dig deeper, to uncover more truths. "As in Rudyard Kipling?"

His eyebrows rise. He tries to cover it up, but I've already seen.

"Are you surprised a stripper has read poetry?" I ask.

"No."

"Liar." I'm not mad though. The girls here are mostly surviving. We're kicking up to the surface. It doesn't leave a lot of leisure time for reading. "So, your parents were fans?"

"Just my mother, as far as I know." He gives a rueful smile like I've disarmed him. Which only proves he came here armed. "I'm just glad I got Kipling and not Rudyard."

I like him this way. More open. Less threatening. It eases me enough that I run my hands down his chest, drawing a shudder from him. "Did you grow up with Mowgli and Baloo?"

"Until I was sick of them," he says. "I had a big book, the kind you can only find in a garage sale. The paper yellow and the binding turning to string."

"It sounds lovely." My hands play lower—at the flat, hard plane at the bottom of his abs. Strippers often chat up the customers. Some of them come for more than a rub down. They want to talk, to flirt. They want to use us like therapists and then fuck us after. It's a kind of foreplay.

I tell myself that's why I'm talking to this man. No other reason. Not because I want to.

"It was," he says, "at the time. I'd get lost in them. I wanted to go live in the jungle."

"And then you grew up and realized you were already there."

His smile is pleased and sly. He likes this. "Is that where we are? The jungle?"

"The ground is made of concrete and the trees are full of glass. But there are snakes here. There are hunters."

"I thought it was just a story," he says lightly.

"Stories are powerful." They're life and death. They're survival. There wasn't much to do locked up in my room except read. And dance. I am a world away from that life, but that still holds true. I still spend most of my time reading and dancing.

And I'm still locked up, in a different way.

He looks too curious for my comfort. "So what stories do you tell?" he murmurs.

I shrug, for all the world nonchalant. "Same old story. Broken home. Ran away. Now I'm a stripper."

It's a sanitized version of the truth.

He frowns, uncertain, a furrow between his eyes. It makes him look younger than his scruff and his swagger and his size would indicate. Not like he feels sorry for me, though. Instead he looks like I'm a puzzle. Something to figure out.

The VIP room is really a miniature of the Grand. And his lap is my stage. His thighs are solid beneath my ass. I'm sitting, legs spread, arms at my side, chin up— totally open to him. It's dark here, but designed so he can look at my body up close. Except he's not looking at my body. He's looking at my eyes, and it almost takes my breath away, the wildness I glimpse in his.

And I need to take this spotlight off me. "So what do you want, Kip? What do you like?"

Dark lashes hide his eyes. "I'd like your real name."

"It's not for sale." And I'm still not sure why I wanted to tell him. It had almost slipped out. He's like a truth serum to me, and that's the most dangerous thing of all.

"Honey—"

"I'm here because you're paying me," I say, desperate to push him away. Desperate to hide. "Don't forget that."

He looks at me, and I watch his eyes harden. I can see the branches and brambles that he grows between us, feel the thorns where they push me out. He wants to dislike me.

He wants to hate me.

I don't know why, but I recognize the cold, hollow feeling in my gut when he looks at me. And I brace myself.

"You want to know what I like?" His gaze roams leisurely over my body. Then he looks me in the eye. "I want to fuck you, Honey. That's what I'd like."

My eyes fall shut. What is that feeling inside me? Relief? Disgust? It feels almost like gratitude. He wants to fuck, like every other guy wants. He's not here to expose my identity, not here to drag me back. He just wants to get his rocks off.

"That's not for sale either. I'm here to dance, to

shake my tits. To rub them against you. That's it."

His eyes narrow. He doesn't like how crude I'm being. He knows it's a weapon I'm wielding, but he's not injured. He's fighting back. Oh yes, there is something wild left in him. If he were in the jungle now, I'm not so sure he'd be the boy. He's much more likely a panther. Dangerous. A predator. "Hands or mouth, your choice."

"I said no."

"These rooms aren't just for dancing. I know that as well as you."

Yes, these rooms are for more than dancing, but that doesn't mean I do more. I don't have to, especially if I don't like the way the man treats me. That's a rule Ivan has for us. A twisted form of protection. I start to leave, but his hand squeezes the back of my neck. I grow still.

"I'm not going to hurt you," he says quietly.

Fear races through my veins. He's already hurting me, by holding me here when I want to leave. "Then what do you call this?" I whisper.

"Keeping you. For a little while. That's what you're here for, isn't it?"

God. He makes it sound so reasonable. But it's not. I know it's not. If it were any other man, I would have twisted away and run out of the booth. I would have been calling for Blue. We're a long way from the man who told me about poetry and childhood dreams, but I can't forget that he did. He's the same man, light and dark, petal and thorn. "Let me go," I say, my voice wavering, unsteady.

"Hands or mouth," he repeats.

I close my eyes. My eyes burn with unshed tears. I don't want to cry. It's like waving a red flag at men like him. But the hands sliding down my body are surprisingly gentle. Over my abs and down to my…

"What are you doing?" I jerk away, but he's got one hand on my hip.

His eyes are dark, knowing. "If you won't decide, I will."

"I'm not going to blow you," I say, feeling small, like I've lost all control of the situation.

"I didn't tell you to," he says, one hand between my legs. The backs of his fingertips brush over my pussy. The thin strip of fabric over my pussy. "I want to fuck you with my fingers. I want to play with your clit until you come. Or maybe I'll slide my tongue over your pussy until you're crying loud enough for the whole club to hear, hmm? Your choice, Honey."

All the air rushes out of me. I don't know why it's so shocking. A blowjob is way dirtier than what he's asking for. But I've never had a man want to get me off. Typically they'd fumble around with my breasts, then come in my hands. I should tell him no again, like I did before. Blue would back me up. Ivan would protect me in this.

But there's a part of me intrigued by what he's offering. "Why?"

Amusement glints in his eyes. "The usual reasons."

It's so crazy I laugh, and my laugh sounds crazy too.

"I'm not going to come, you know."

He considers this as he turns his hand and cups my pussy. He isn't waiting until we've negotiated a price. He isn't waiting for permission. And I'm letting him. *Oh God.* He finds my clit with his thumb and gently circles.

He trails callused fingertips down my pussy and back up again. Slow. Focused. He seems to be making a study of me, mapping out my body. I've never had anyone go this slow, this careful. Never had hands so large be gentle.

"I wanted to touch you since I first saw you walk onto the stage. Whether I have to pay or not, whether you return the favor or not, I don't give a fuck. I'm going to finger this pretty cunt until you gush all over my hand. I'm going to keep going until you're slick with it, until my jeans are damp with you, until the scent of your sex is in the air."

I stare at him, somehow shocked, as if I've never heard these dirty words or witnessed these dirty acts. And I haven't—not the words in that order. Not with my body reacting, getting tight and wet for him. I think I actually might come for him.

"No," I whisper.

His fingers don't stop stroking me. If anything they slip in deeper. "That's what I want around my dick. Not your hands or your mouth. I want the juice from your pussy. When you're wet and coming, I'm going to dip my fingers inside your pretty pussy. I'll cover my dick with your juices, just like it would be if I fucked you bareback."

I could imagine him then, cock heavy with arousal, glistening with my wetness. His cock would be large, like his hands and his whole body are large.

In the end it isn't his blunt fingers against my clit. Not even the dark, possessive gleam in his eyes. What pushes me over is the clean, earthy scent of him. I lean close, pressing my nose to his neck and breathing in deep as I come.

I stay there, pressed into every hollow place in him, somehow finding solace in the hard angles of his body. He is a mountain, and I am the shadows that fill every nook and cave around him.

Reality comes back to me, along with embarrassment. And confusion. I've never come in this room. Never in this building. God, I haven't even masturbated in forever—so worn down from hiding, so shamed by the place I'm hiding in, this strip club.

I'm hiding in him now.

How did he do this to me? One hour ago I had never seen this man, never imagined getting turned on in this dank room. Never sought comfort against rough, whisker-ticklish skin. He's changing me, teaching me to want more than survival.

Dangerous.

"Okay?" he asks, voice gruff.

Maybe he can tell I'm emotional. But if he thinks I need to feel dead inside to do my job, he's wrong. Lola is the strong one, the one who performs without feeling a thing. Candy does it too, even if she needs drugs to manage it. But I've never been able to find that numbness. I feel it all—every insult, every grope. Every cock. And now I would feel his thick cock too.

That doesn't seem like the worst thing.

"How do you want me?" My voice trembles, but that doesn't stop him.

His fingers are cupping my pussy, unmoving, letting me recover. Now he dips his finger inside, where I am the most sensitive and wet. Then he lifts his hand to my mouth. One stroke, painting my lips with my arousal, heating up every nerve ending. His head dips, and I know what's coming next. But I don't turn my face away. I don't tell him kisses aren't for sale.

I let him taste me on my lips. He licks the wetness, a slow swipe of his tongue that makes me gasp. My lips part, and he takes full advantage. His tongue pushes inside, opening me. His hand at the back of my neck is my only anchor while his mouth claims mine.

It's almost too much. Too intense.

"*How do you want me?*" I'm demanding this time. I need to know. Because I need to stop this strange intimacy that only increases with every murmured word and tender touch.

"What are you afraid of, sweetheart?"

My eyes widen. How does he know?

Maybe he's not really that perceptive. Maybe all the men that come through here can see I'm terrified, but they don't care as long as I make them hard.

"How do you want me?" My voice is hoarse, pleading. *This is all I have to give. Take it.*

His jaw tightens. "I want you like this. Spread open. Waiting for me to do whatever I want to you."

His hand returns to my pussy, and I feel relief. Disappointment too. It hurts that he's stopped kissing me, because for some reason I liked it. And I know, most likely, it won't happen again. Not tonight. Not ever again. But it's for the best. I shouldn't get used to this.

He pulls more wetness from my core and paints my nipples—first one, then the other. I shiver under his touch. It's more like shaking, really. Because I know what comes next, the same thing he did to my mouth.

He pulls me up so my breasts are in front of his face. He licks the wetness off my nipple, sucks me until I moan. Then he gives my other breast the same treatment.

And I can't say anything. Can't demand to know how he wants me. He dips his fingers one more time, deep inside me, pulling out all the wetness he can find. I clench around his fingers and hear his breath catch.

He doesn't put my arousal on my body, not this time. Slowly, deliberately, he unbuckles his pants and pulls himself out. He's as hard as I imagined. As big. As slick at the tip. He runs a fist down his length, mixing my arousal with his precum over his cock.

I can't say anything, but I don't have to. *How do you want me?* I know how he wants me, and I slide to the floor. The floor that's cold and dusty and damp at the same time, unforgiving against my shins. I'm more comfortable here. Safer. Because this *is* for sale. And I have the upper hand now. Sex is a battlefield, and this concrete floor is my country to defend.

"What's your name?" His voice is low—and desperate? That can't be right. He doesn't need anything from me. He could have gone to a bar. With that hard jaw and hard body, he would have had his pick. Any girl would have hopped on the back of the motorcycle I suspect he has. And yet he's here.

He can pay for my mouth. He can even pay for my orgasms. He doesn't get my name.

"Honey."

He laughs, a little coarse, a little bitter. But his eyes, they understand. They're almost soft, tender as they look down at me kneeling. "Pretty little liar."

But when I lean forward to take him in my mouth, he pushes me away. He fists his cock, fucking himself, still slick from my pussy. He's taking himself fast and hard—almost like a punishment.

He took his time with me, but not with himself. Now he races himself to the finish line, fist and hips at war until he tenses and comes, spilling into his own hand while I kneel before him and watch.

He collapses back onto the chair, still sprawled but truly relaxed now. Not tense or wary. Not carefully banked power like I felt before. Now he is an animal in repose, a lion spread across a rock, bathing in the sun— even if the rock is a creaking wooden chair, straining under his force. Even if the sun is the flicker of fluorescent lights from the edges of the velvet curtain. It's still primal.

Still beautiful.

His eyes are closed. His head falls back.

And for some reason I almost tell him my name. I form it with my lips and tongue, but he can't see. I don't know why I'd ever tell him…except that I want someone to see me here. To know me here. So that I don't have to feel alone.

But he isn't here to know me. He isn't here to save me either.

Alertness breathes into him again. His expression is sated and…grateful. "C'mere," he says on a grunt.

And before I can do what he says, he lifts me into his lap. He tucks my legs over the side of his and kisses me—slow, languid swipes of his tongue against mine.

I push away from him, staggering back. I don't have my balance yet, but it doesn't matter. I shove aside the velvet curtain and run. He hasn't paid me, but I don't care.

"What the hell?" Blue asks, grabbing my arm.

But I break free and keep running. I don't care what happens behind me. I don't care about Kip or the fact that I'll never see him again.

It's better if I don't.

I read my mother's diary until the day she left. That's how I knew about her affair with the guards. More than one, although it was the last man who got her killed. She thought she loved him.

And she was planning to leave my father.

In that diary I saw her ticket to Tanglewood, West Virginia. There were two words scrawled on the ticket— *The Grand.* I'd never heard of it then, but it became a kind of North Star for me. As a teenager I had to stay with my family.

And when I'd finally run, I'd known just where we'd go.

I just hadn't known it was a strip club until I arrived.

CHAPTER THREE

A STRANGER LOOKS at me from the mirror.

Black thong and red lipstick. They're my costume, but sometimes it feels like I don't need them. I've been hiding long enough that it feels more natural than honesty. My green eyes and black hair and pale skin are a costume too. I use them to disguise myself when I strip—just another set of tits and ass. How deep does that costume go?

Is there anything underneath?

I'm not sure anymore.

Lola crosses the room toward me. I watch her in the mirror, even when she perches on my vanity table. She wears some kind of red-leather strap bodice that shows more skin than it covers. It looks sexy and almost alien. "What happened?" she asks.

I blink. "What do you mean?"

"Don't play dumb. That's Candy's routine. I know something's eating you. And I know you left early last night. Some guy get fresh?"

Yeah, some guy had gotten fresh. But it had happened before and never affected me like this. It's a good sign that she doesn't know what happened though. It means Blue probably collected the money and made excuses for me. I'll owe him one now. "I wasn't feeling well."

Her expression is knowing—and sympathetic. It's the sympathy that hurts the most. "If you want to talk about it…"

I don't want to talk about Kip and how strange he made me feel. Lola doesn't even know why I'm here, who I'm running from—and I want to keep it that way. She doesn't know any of my secrets.

"Where's Candy?" I say instead.

"*If you want to talk about it,*" she says more sternly, "I'm here. The offer stands. And anyway, maybe there's something going around, because Candy didn't show today either."

But Lola and I both know there isn't any real sickness. "Did she call in?"

"No, but you know Candy."

I do know Candy. I know she sometimes goes home with guys who promise her a good time, even though Ivan has rules about that. I know for Candy *a good time* means alcohol or drugs or both. It's a dangerous game she plays, but I can't judge. I just worry. "Maybe we can stop by after our shift."

Lola snorts. "And get attacked in that fucking rat trap she lives in? No, thanks. I'd rather get attacked here. At least then I get paid."

All the girls live in crappy places, but Candy's place is actually the worst. Part of the ceiling in the hallway has just caved in, and there are always guys sitting in the stairwells. It looks more like an abandoned building that squatters use.

I kind of can't believe she pays to live there. "Maybe if she doesn't show up tomorrow, we'll go."

"She'd better show up tomorrow. Ivan's already pissed."

Shit shit shit.

Dread forms a large knot in my stomach. Ivan is our boss, and the second-scariest man I've ever met. Maybe Blue did tell on me. Though Ivan doesn't visit often, and it seemed weird that he'd come just because I'd left early. And also acted strange with a customer, running out before getting paid. But even if I wasn't the reason for his visit, I still might get in trouble now that he's here.

Another part of me tensed in anticipation. Maybe he had information for me.

"Ivan's here?"

"Just talked to him in his office." Lola winks. "Oh, did I not mention? He wants to see you."

IF THE GRAND is the murky underwater, then the basement office is the sea bottom, far enough down that no light can reach. The railing keeps me from tripping and falling down the stairs. At the small landing, I knock on the door and wait.

There's a framed painting of the Grand hanging on the wall. Its brick was once a deep, startling red. For some reason, the painting hasn't faded, entombed here in the basement. But the real brick did fade. It turned dark the way blood does when it dries. That's all the building is to the city now—a scab.

A minute passes, and then I hear Ivan inside. "Enter."

When I go inside, it's the opposite of a stage. There are no spotlights to blind me. Just a dim stillness to wade through. The room is mostly unfinished, with a concrete floor and exposed vents from the ceiling. It's the kind of place where I wouldn't be surprised to find a person hanging in chains in the corner. A dungeon.

There have never been chains down here. I have an overactive imagination.

Or maybe a good memory, of a different time and place.

"Mr. Kosta," I say.

"Sit." He doesn't look up from the paper he's reading.

I'm not sure how the small lamp provides enough light to see by, but he's absorbed in his work. Then his gaze flicks to me, and I understand. Because his pale blue eyes are like spotlights, making me feel exposed.

"How are you, Honey?"

I suppress a shiver.

The first time we met, I came to him for a favor. I needed information. Why had my mother planned to come here? What was waiting for her here? And some small part of me still hoped she'd arrived, that she'd escaped some other way.

Ivan had made me dance for him.

He watched me impassively. The hardness in his suit pants told me he liked what he saw, but his eyes were flat. He made no comment on my body, made no move to touch me. Instead he said I would work at his club. I would only have to dance. Not fuck anyone. And in return he would look for the information I needed. He was the most well-connected man in this old city.

And he named me Honey. Similar to my own name, but the opposite really.

I hate the name, and I think he knows that. It's a hammer. Every time I hear it, I sink a little deeper into the wood.

I think he knows that too.

"Fine, sir," I say now.

That earns me a faint smile. "So respectful. Are you this respectful with everyone?"

Yes. I've always been the good girl. "I don't know."

I remember avoiding Blue's gaze. I remember kneeling at Kip's feet. I probably do look respectful, but mostly I feel afraid. Maybe those are the same things.

"Do you know why I called you down?"

I shake my head, hopeful. "You found something?"

"Yes." He leans back and crosses one ankle over his knee. "But that's not the only reason. Someone was asking about you."

My throat seems to close up entirely. I can almost hear the metal clang of a gate falling around me, trapping me where I sit. He already knows way more about me than is safe. I had to tell him in order to stay here. Had to tell him to get the information I need. Had to tell him to keep my sister safe. *Clara.*

If he tells someone else, I'm fucked. And so is she.

"Who? When? What did you tell them?" My words come out soft, almost like a shuddery breath. That's all I can do now. Count my breaths and stare down the barrel.

"I told them you're one of my girls." One corner of his mouth lifts. "I told them you're valuable to me. And loyal. Aren't you?"

All I can think about is running again. That's the opposite of loyalty. "Yes."

He laughs softly. "You're a nice girl. A good girl. You've always done what I need you to. I like to reward good behavior."

Does he mean information? Protection? The former is why I'm here. But the latter… God, we need protection. I can't imagine he would do that. No matter how much I earn onstage, it isn't worth using his resources to guard me. No, I can't rely on Ivan.

We've been found. We're in danger. My mind is already mapping bus routes out of the city. Where would I go next? Far. That's the answer.

As far as the money I'd earned stripping would last.

He looks thoughtful. "You'll be safe enough here. His name is Kip. And I think…" A smile now. "I think he wants to fuck you."

Relief pours through me, so hot and potent I feel faint with it. I can't even be angry that Ivan has been taunting me with this. It's not Byron. It's not my father. It's just a man interested in a stripper—*nothing special here, move along.* "I've danced for him."

Ivan's eyes narrow. "Interesting. Actually, I found something you might be interested in. In my own records. It turns out the man you asked about used to work here. Security. This was before I came to own the place. From the file I have, he'd been fucking around with the girls one time too many."

I flinch. That is the man my mother had believed herself in love with. That is who she'd gotten killed for. "When did he stop working here?"

Ivan reads off a date from a paper on his desk.

I imagine this man getting fired and looking for work elsewhere. He could have gotten a job with my father in a different state. He had fallen in love with my mother— or at least pretended to. They'd hatched the plan to steal the jewels. He never could have pulled it off alone. My mother would have helped him.

An inside job all the way.

A few days later my father told me she was in a car accident, even though she wasn't allowed to leave the mansion any more than I was. She certainly wasn't allowed to drive herself. It was clearly a lie, but what was he hiding? Her murder? Or her escape?

A man with his pride might have said that to save face. I'm here because of simple, stupid hope. Maybe she did use that ticket to leave Las Vegas. Maybe she's still alive. Maybe she's living in a cute little house with her lover—with spare bedrooms for me and Clara.

Okay, that last part is just a fantasy. But there's something here in this city. The jewels? The truth? I need to find out if my mother made it here. I need to find out what happened to her.

"My mother?" I ask.

He shakes his head. *No. Not yet.*

And I need to keep stripping if I want him to keep looking.

"Can I go now?" I whisper. It's a weakness, I know that. If I were stronger, I could bluff. I'd pretend I didn't care and walk out with a flick of my hair, like Candy can do.

I'm not bluffing though. I can't. My whole body is a tell—tense and terrified.

"Why would I keep you?" The question isn't innocent. He doesn't mean *I'd never keep a woman against her will.* He means, *You're valuable to me. I can use you.* His casual tone is a block of cheese set inside a trap, something to lure me inside. I'm a mouse in a lion's den. He's playing with me. It's only a matter of time until he pounces. But if I leave the cave, I give up any chance of keeping Clara safe.

We'd be found eventually, but we wouldn't have the leverage to fight my father.

My chest is tight. "I'm doing what you asked me to. Dancing." *Fucking.*

In that, he's just like Byron. Just like my father. They want my body. They want vacant eyes and a small clay smile. They want a doll.

He nods, accepting my obedience as if it's his due. "And I'll keep looking for information on your mother. But I want you to stay away from Kip."

What? I stare back, silent. It's bad enough to have to dance for these men at the flick of his fingers. Now I have to stop. There's something deeper going on here. Why does he know Kip but dislike him? He seems almost afraid... and yet, he's the most dangerous man here.

So what does that make Kip?

Ivan smiles, predatory. "It's interesting that he's here at all, but then you're an interesting woman. I knew that the first time I saw you, when you showed up desperate for a job and much too thin. But you certainly know how to make the customers hard, don't you, Honor?"

I flinch, more because he uses my real name than anything else.

I can't deny that I was desperate. I'd have done anything for this job, but Ivan's never fucked me, never touched me. He's never watched me dance beyond the initial interview I did for him. In that respect I've been lucky to be here. But I know male appreciation when I see it. If I have to use that to stay off the grid, I will. If I have to use it to save Clara, I will.

After all, that's what I've been doing all this time.

"I'll do anything." I'm not even sure what I'm begging for. Answers? Sanctuary?

But he seems to know. His eyebrows rise. "How about giving me your sister?" A beat. "No? I didn't think so."

I swallow hard. He doesn't want my sister, not really. He wants me desperate.

And that's what he'll get.

I can do this. Hadn't I just done the same thing last night? But it feels different, when I stand up. It feels different because when I did this to Kip, I wanted to. No matter what I told myself, it hadn't been fear I'd felt behind that velvet curtain. Not fear of him, anyway. I'd felt desire, and that was the scariest thing of all.

I don't feel desire now, but I still know how to move my hips, how to kneel in front of him, how to run a hand across his thigh. His legs part to give me access, but I need more permission before I can continue. Overstepping my bounds with a man like him can be fatal.

"Let me," I whisper.

Let me touch him, suck him. *Let me go.*

He catches my chin between his thumb and forefinger, forcing me to look him in the eye—in a similar position to what Kip had been in last night. But Kip's dark eyes had been hungry and warm and concerned.

Ivan just looks curious, as if I were an animal performing some mating act he finds faintly distasteful. "If you suck me off, what then? You'll walk out that door, and I'll lose one of my best dancers."

I flinch, unable to deny the truth.

If he let me go now, I'd be gone. On the run, again and always. But if Ivan has figured that out, then he won't let me go. My stomach turns over.

He smiles. "I want something far more valuable than a blowjob, Honor. I want you. Here. And under my control. So don't bother running. I'd only find you. Unless the person you're running from finds you first."

I stand to leave. I'd have run if I needed to. I'd have fought if he made me. But he leans back in his chair, apparently content to let me go for now. I hurry to the door.

"Oh, and Honey?"

I pause, feeling small. He knows. *He likes it that way.*

"Kip and I go way back. Let's just say, he's not someone you want to fuck with."

Oh, and you are? I just nod briefly—a jerk of my head. Acknowledging the truth of it.

"Stay away from him," he says. It's not a suggestion. It's an order.

CHAPTER FOUR

I IMAGINE MYSELF on a bus heading somewhere far away. Except if I leave, I know Ivan will find me. And in the process, he'll kick over every rock until *everyone* knows where to find me. I'm trapped just as surely as when I left. Unless I stay here and keep my head down, earn more money, stay safe another few days…and maybe find out what happened to my mother. Doesn't she deserve justice? Doesn't she deserve peace?

Clara deserves it, that's for sure. Finding those jewels means peace. It's a long shot, but so is staying alive. Survival is a long shot when you have dangerous men hunting you. And dangerous men ordering you around.

Ivan ordered me to stay away from Kip, but somehow I'm standing here in front of the velvet curtain. I'm wearing full gear tonight for the floor. That means a lacy black bra and panties, just begging to be ripped off in front of some panting guy, in the dark recesses of a VIP room. I feel shaky, like I might throw up. It's not stage fright. It's the opposite. I can dance in front of a roomful of men. But the thought of being enclosed with this one is making my heart pound.

I glance back, but Blue is busy with some guy who

got too up close and personal with Lola. I could wait for him to be finished and then tell him Ivan won't let me see this guy. Blue isn't about to disobey an order like that. But on some level I don't want Blue to step in. I don't want to listen to Ivan.

I want to go inside.

My palms grow hot. I know he'll be sprawled on the chair, one long leg kicked out, the other tucked back. I know he'll be wearing the scuffed boots and leather jacket. I know exactly how he'll smell—like musk and danger, like salt and spice.

When I slip past the curtain, a slow grin spreads across his face. It looks like a smile I'd see when I open the door for a date, both appreciative and a little surprised. It should be out of place in the dark, dank VIP room, but my heart flutters anyway.

Damn it. I'm determined to make this time different.

"Hey, sugar," I say in a voice so smooth and practiced it is clearly false. "I'm glad to see you."

He doesn't need to know that I actually am glad to see him again. Or that I find him sexy.

His smile fades a little. Apparently the seductress play isn't what he's expecting. Last time I'd been bumbling and awkward and, worst of all, real. I won't make that mistake twice.

He studies me like I'm a puzzle. *I'm the simplest thing you'll ever see,* I want to tell him. *I'm afraid.* But I smile instead. It's not a big smile, not real, but it's pretty. I know exactly what it looks like in the mirror, with my makeup on. I give it to him the same way I give him my time and my body—by the hour.

"What'll it be tonight, sugar?" I ask.

A little crease forms between his eyebrows. My fingers twitch. I want to smooth it away. And then I'd keep going, running my fingertip over those thick eyebrows, trailing my hand down his bristly cheek. I shave and pluck the hairs on my body, leaving my skin smooth. But he has all his hair—he's covered in the stuff. It looks both soft and coarse, both attractive and forbidding.

"Can I talk to you?" he asks quietly.

This was what I'd been afraid of. Niceness. Curiosity. It's not good, coming from a customer. It's not good coming from anyone. "We're talking right now, sugar."

"Come here." He pulls his leg even, making it clear he wants me on his lap. I remember that lap, his thighs strong and warm and thick under me. I had an orgasm on that lap.

I can't risk it. So I slide to the floor instead, glancing up at him with a seductive smile. My breasts sway as I crawl toward him in the small space. I move like a cat, rubbing against him before flicking my ass. His gaze roams my body, hovering on each part, unable to choose a place to land. He likes my breasts and my belly, my ass and my legs.

Then he looks back at my face, locking his eyes on mine. "I said come here."

He doesn't let me get away with much. I can feel the invisible leash around my neck. I can feel him tug. I slip between his legs. It's close enough to his lap that I can pretend innocence. Maybe this was what he meant all along. I give lap dances all night long, but very few men will turn down a blowjob if I'm already kneeling between their legs.

I slide my hands up his thighs, staring at the bulge in his jeans. He wants this, and somehow so do I. I don't have any illusions about blowjobs. I don't imagine it will taste good or feel sexy, but I want to hear him fall apart. I want to feel it.

His hands grab my wrists. His eyes are dark now, displeased.

He pulls. My body swings up, easy and lightweight in his arms. Then I'm in his lap, tucked into the crook of his arm, straddling his legs. *Shit.*

I force myself to pout, to keep things lighthearted. "I want to make you feel good, sugar."

His arms tighten around me, half embrace and half prison. "You do."

My heart pounds. He pushes past my defenses, just like that. Not with cruelty. That I could manage. Or at least, survive. He slips underneath my walls just by looking at them. I don't know what would happen if he actually did more. How quickly I would fall.

And I want him to feel just as vulnerable—more. So I relax my body, as if I'm giving in. I rest my arms on his shoulders, either side. My palms slide down his chest to frame the necklace he wears, the one underneath his shirt.

"What's this?" I whisper.

His expression closes. "It's nothing."

I recognize those walls—I put them up myself. And I recognize those lies. They are all I have left. That alone should make me respect his wishes. I can suck his dick without lifting his shirt. Instead I find myself stroking his neck, reaching down to the warm metal chain—and pulling out the necklace.

A cross. A simple cross with straight lines, formed out of a black stone with cloudy white swirling through. Marble? I think he must have worn it for a long time. But somehow I know I am one of the only people to ever see it.

Because he let me see it. I don't fool myself. He could have stopped me. He could do *anything* to me, but he let me take out his necklace. The unexpected trust sits on my chest, making it hard to breathe.

"I didn't take you for a religious man." It isn't only his presence here in the strip club. Hypocrisy runs deep. I wouldn't be surprised to find half the men here in church on Sundays, wiping away their sins with the same hands and tongues they used to defile me.

But he has something they don't, a kind of fight, a stark determination that says he walks his own path. He has his own plan—and no use for God's.

"I'm not religious," he says, tucking the cross back under his shirt. "That's a gift."

It has to be from a woman. While the shape of it is simple, almost primitive, it was clearly chosen with love and feminine affection. And it certainly matches Kip's dark looks—his black boots and black jacket. His black eyes. They're angry now, but I don't stop. A wise woman would leave him alone. She would take her clothes off. She'd give him her body. But she'd never trust him with her heart.

"Who gave this to you?" I whisper. His mother? A girlfriend?

His wife?

I tell myself it doesn't matter. Plenty of men here are married. Rings are common enough, worn by men too lazy or brazen to take them off before coming. But I don't want this man to be married.

His expression darkens. "You want answers, but you won't give me any. Fair's fair, sweetheart."

I flinch as his hand reaches for me, but he only tucks a lock of hair behind my ear. It's always coming undone from the pins I use to hold it. My hair is always falling down around me, tumbling and wild. The admiration in his eyes says he likes it that way. His hand lingers in my hair, teasing the strands between his fingers.

"Tell me your name," he says gently. "If you don't trust me, I can't help you."

Every muscle freezes. Cold sweeps in, turning me to ice. I don't feel fear. I can't feel pain. "How do you know I need help?"

His eyes soften. The understanding in them is like a physical blow, and I have to hold my breath just to keep myself from shattering.

"Don't you?" He strokes rough fingers down my cheek. "Your eyes ask for help. Your body. You look down at me from the stage like you want me to climb up and take you away."

I stare at him, shocked. Shocked that he read so much into me. Shocked that he's right. "*No.*"

His large hand wraps the back of my neck. He tugs me close and whispers in my ear, "What are you afraid of?"

My heart pounds so loud it's all I can hear. The dark walls become blurry as if I'm going fast instead of trapped. As if I'm falling. "I don't need your help. This is where I want to be."

He looks around like he's just noticed our surroundings. Sharp eyes don't miss anything—not the grit on the floor or the desolation in my lie. "This is where you want to be," he says. "This hellhole. Is that right?"

I laugh suddenly. It takes me by surprise. "This isn't hell. You think heaven is nice clothes and expensive locks? That's what hell is made of."

Then there's knowledge in his eyes. "And you left that…for this."

"I don't need your pity." It makes me angry, the way he's looking at me. I don't want him to feel sorry for me. I want him to desire me again. I want to see him panting after me again. "What I need is for you to stop talking and start fucking. You can do that, right? That's what you're here for, isn't it?"

His hand tightens in my hair. For a moment I think

he's going to call my bluff. In that moment, I want him to. Instead he tugs downward, guiding me to the floor.

Now he'll fuck my mouth, won't he? He'll use me, just like I wanted.

But he doesn't do that.

Instead he pushes his boot between my legs. His hand remains in my hair, holding me there. I'm straddling his leg, bracing myself with my hands on his thighs. Is he going to... kick me? But there isn't really room for that. There isn't room for much of anything, except the solid warmth of his leg holding me up. I've had my legs spread, my ass up, my mouth around a stranger's cock—but I've never felt quite as vulnerable as I do now.

"What are you going to do to me?" My voice trembles. I can't even find it in me to care. Pride is a thing of the past. Pride is silk and good wine—things I can no longer afford.

"What you asked for." He looks angry now, but his touch is still gentle as he shifts me lower. I'm hugging his leg now, the warm leather of his boot pressed right against my pussy. "You wanted us to fuck. You wanted me to pay you for it. Well, this is how I want you."

A pain in my scalp drags me up, and then I'm rocking back down again. Up and then down—he gives me the rhythm to move. It's sex, that rhythm.

It's dancing.

I'm already in a strip club. There should be nothing dirtier I can do, nothing lower. But now I'm grinding on this man's boot, feeling horrible pleasure spark in my clit, and I realize I was wrong. This is worse. This is dirtier by far.

"Wait," I whimper even though I don't know what we'd wait for.

His hand drops, heavy on my shoulder, squeezing gently. "No, baby. This is what you asked for, and I'm giving it to you. That's how this works."

"This isn't..." My throat feels tight, and horrible tears prick my eyes. I didn't cry when I danced onstage the first time. Didn't cry when I got fucked. Why does he make me feel like this? It's even worse than how Byron made me feel. "This isn't using me. It's not making you feel good."

A rough laugh, like metal dragging over concrete. "Oh, I'm feeling pretty good, sweetheart."

He means his erection. He means the sizable bulge in his jeans.

"Let me stroke you," I beg him. Anything would be easier than getting raked over his boot, fucking his leg, exposed in my own awkward arousal. It's building even though I know this is wrong. No, it's building faster *because* it's so wrong. There's something perverse in me. I don't know if I was born with it or if Byron drilled it into me, but the humiliation only makes me hotter. Every stroke of the supple leather to my clit brings a new rush of heat.

He shakes his head, the expression in his eyes almost sad. "This is what you asked for," he repeats. "Maybe next time you'll ask for what you need."

I shudder, right on the edge. "I need, I need—"

"I know," he murmurs.

As I look into his eyes, I have the strangest feeling that he *does* know. Maybe he already knows what I'm afraid of. Maybe he knows what I need. It pushes me over, and then I'm coming, rocking my clit against leather, humping his leg while he murmurs how good I am, how sweet.

And when I am done, my body trembling, heart thudding, he pays me. I stare at the money as if I've never seen it before—as if I've never gotten paid before. As if it's never hurt this bad before.

His expression is hungry as he stares down at me. But I must not be enough, because his erection is still thick in his jeans when he stands.

He looks down at me, and I feel again those brambles grow wild and fast, foliage too dense to see past, branches too thick to cut down. And again, that strange sense that he wants to hate me. He doesn't want to get close. I remember this feeling too well. And when Kip leaves, I shiver on the floor, nauseous and afraid, remembering.

✦ ✦ ✦

Six months ago

MY FACE IS stiff from smiling. My calves ache from the four-inch heels. Why is it the more a shoe costs, the thinner its sole? I greet another couple with as much warmth as I can pretend, considering the man has a lipstick smear on his face.

Not the same shade as his wife's lipstick.

These parties are see and be seen. Fuck and be fucked. The woman scans the room as we discuss the latest charity fundraiser. She's looking for her next conquest.

"Honor, darling." The voice is like a cube of ice all the way down my spine.

I turn to greet the handsome man. Byron Adams, my fiancé. And the rising star in the Las Vegas Police Department. He's aiming for police commissioner. "Byron, I was wondering where you'd gotten to."

There is no lipstick on his face, which isn't proof of anything. No, the main reason I believe he is faithful is because of the look in his eye. The one that scares me. "I was talking business," he says with an almost bashful smile. It was strange to see that expression on him. It made him seem younger. It made me ache. "And missing you."

Both the man and woman smile at us like we're in love. I have to remember that. We *are* in love.

I lay my hand on his arm and force a smile. "Then take me with you."

And he does. He leads me out of the room and up the stairs to the office. I've been in this office a thousand times, but not like this. Not with my fiancé's rough hands bending me over the desk. He drags up the hem of my glittery dress, exposing my ass. The thong snaps.

"I couldn't find you," he says, voice tight.

There's no right answer. If he wants me, he gets me. "I'm sorry," I murmur, pleading.

The sound of a zipper pierces the room. Then he is inside me, skin to skin. His cock thrusts deep into my cunt. The papers are probably important, the tally of millions of dollars, but I crush them in my fists.

His fingers dig into my hips. "I don't like that. Stay where I can see you."

"I will," I gasp out, but it's hard. Hard because I can barely breathe, the way he's thrusting faster now. Harder. The way my face is shoved into the desk, leaving streaks of eye makeup on the crinkled sheets of paper, damp with tears.

We are in love.

He pulls out. I tense up, knowing what's coming next. If I'd had any doubts—any hopes—they are gone when he spits onto my ass. Careless fingers smooth the saliva into my puckered hole. Then his cock is pressing against me.

I practice like he tells me to. The plugs are as big as I can bear, but it's still too much. Too much when his cock is inside me, dragging against the tender flesh, fucking me.

"Wait," I whimper. "Wait."

I don't mean *wait.* I mean *no no no.* I mean *stop and never start again.* It doesn't matter. He doesn't stop, and that's for the best. If he did, he'd ask what I meant. He'd ask why I said it. And I don't have answers for him. I only have my own muffled groans as he slams back into me.

I only have pain as he presses deep.

CHAPTER FIVE

THE REST OF the night I dance in a kind of trance, only vaguely aware of the flashing lights or the applause. The hands that reach for me, stroking and grabbing, barely register tonight. The hurt and shame I feel after being made to fuck his boot are too strong. I can see why Candy likes to shoot up before she goes onstage. I wish she was here so I could ask her for a hit.

There's shock too, and that helps.

It's dreamlike. I'm not really here, undressing and shaking my ass for strangers. I'm not even awake.

The sky is already a murky orange by the time I leave. A fine mist hangs between the buildings, a cross between fog and morning dew. The Grand is closing. Blue is ejecting the last customers, and they wander away, tripping their way over the uneven cobblestones, bleary and already hungover. Half the stones in the driveway are gone, pieces of the building's façade missing, as if we're in some battle-torn country. And we are. Wars are fought and lost on this street.

The well of the central fountain contains only dried leaves and cigarette butts. Whatever statuette once adorned the center pillar has long since been cracked off, leaving only a jagged edge jutting up. It's a fitting centerpiece for the courtyard and the Grand as a whole, broken and proud.

I'm still in a trance as I head to Candy's apartment. The numbness helps me here too, dulling my fear as I step over the bums and scary-looking men slumped over in the stairwell.

My knock echoes off the faded green walls.

She doesn't answer.

"Candy," I say, pressing my face against the door, hoping she'll hear me. Still no answer. I try the doorknob just in case, but it's locked.

Worry churns in my stomach. If she OD'ed on something behind that door...if she went home with some guy and he tied her up in the basement... there are so many ways she could get into trouble. So many ways to get hurt.

I know that from experience.

"Candy." This time it's a whisper. I know she won't answer. Whether she's high or just gone, she's beyond my reach.

Silly to think I could help her, when I can't even help myself.

I climb over the men on the stairs, hopeless and distracted. I almost don't notice the man who holds the door open for me. In fact I'm already turning toward the sidewalk outside Candy's apartment when I feel the prickle on the back of my neck. The same one I felt the first night he showed up at the strip club.

I freeze. Every muscle in my body locks tight.

"I'm not going to hurt you," comes a masculine murmur behind me. A *familiar* male voice.

My heart pounds. My hands clench around the handle of the duffel bag.

"Honey," he says softly. And there's none of the mocking this time, even though the name is fake. He sounds mostly concerned.

Oh God, it's him. I'd hoped I was wrong. He may say he's not going to hurt me, but no man shows up uninvited to a stripper's room with good intentions. I don't turn, don't face him. I speak to the empty sidewalk instead. "What are you doing here?"

"I followed you." He pauses. "It's not safe here."

A chill runs over my skin. How did I miss him? And what else have I missed? Time on the run has given me certain skills, but I'm not a spy. I'm an heiress. A *principessa*. At least that's what I was trained to be. I can host a dinner party for the most wealthy, lethal men in the country, but I don't know how to spot a tail. I don't know how to fight one.

I swallow hard. "What do you want from me?"

A blowjob? A fuck? These are the only things I have to give.

His sigh caresses my temple, gently ruffling my hair. "I just want to talk."

That makes me scoff. He may stalk me, and I may fuck him, but at least we can be honest about it. "Then why are you in my space?"

Politeness is a ten-dollar bill tossed onto the stage. But for this, stalking and holding open the door in a parody of gentlemanly manners, he can get out of my personal space. He can stop making my heart beat too fast and my skin feel clammy and hot.

After a pause, he steps back. Not far, but enough that I can breathe again. I turn to face him—and again I'm struck with that sense of déjà vu, of recognition. Have I met him before? I would remember that face, the hardness of his features, the hint of vulnerability in his dark eyes, but all I have is a strange feeling, like I trust him even though he's a stranger.

Obviously it's a feeling I can't trust.

I consider running for it, as useless as that would be. He's too fast for me. And I don't want to see what he's like when he gets rough. And besides, I'd run the risk of leading him to the motel room—and to Clara.

It's not like I could call the cops on him—at least not without answering a lot of other uncomfortable questions. Instead I let him ease the duffel bag away from me when he moves to take it from me. Without asking, of course. He slings it over his shoulder in a dark parallel to chivalry. He'll let me go when he's ready to.

"I'm not going to hurt you." His gaze remains on me as we stand in front of Candy's shit-hole apartment building. This building, this ground had seen violence before. I can feel it vibrate through the concrete. And it probably will again—I just hope it won't be today.

I press my hands together, hating how helpless I feel.

"Then let's walk. In public."

When he doesn't answer, I head back toward the club. He falls in step beside me.

Public is a generous term for the street. No one would come running to help if I screamed. But it's better than letting him follow me home. A whole lot better.

"Relax," he says, somewhat dry and almost sad. "If I wanted to fuck you, I'd have met you in the club."

And if he'd wanted to kill me, he could have done it a hundred times by now. He'd followed me here. I'm still alive. But I can't relax. Not while I'm wondering whether he followed me any other night and what he saw. Who he saw. "Plenty of guys would like a freebie."

Has he followed me home? I have to assume he hasn't. I have to believe she's safe, otherwise there's no point to any of this.

"I'll always pay," he says, and I know he's teasing a little. But a little bit not. "Cross my heart."

It's more than money now. It's also distance. He's drawing a line in the sand. He's telling me he needs that line just as much as I do. "And tip," I add. Because I can tease too.

His smile always dawns like the morning, slow and warm, wiping away the night's chill. "Not *just* the tip, though."

Oh my God. I roll my eyes, but I'm smiling too. "So what did you want to talk about?"

"Lots of things," he says, catching my hand. "Like who you're afraid of."

I flinch. I'm afraid of Byron. I'm afraid of my father. I'm afraid of everyone. "What makes you think I'm afraid?"

"I know a girl in trouble when I see one. And you're it."

"So you're here to save the day?" More likely he'd get himself killed. Yeah, the man is obviously tough—but my father has a fucking army at his command. Kip should find some other girl to stalk and harass. A different one to use. He should find a different girl to protect. "I can't be what you want."

A grim smile flickers over his face. "You really don't know what I want, sweetheart. You'd be a lot more scared if you did."

✧   ✧   ✧

Six months ago

I'M STILL FACEDOWN on the desk, being pounded, when I hear the door open. I tense. What if it's a guest? But then I hear the cadence of my father's gait—one light step, one heavy, one creak of his cane.

Oh God. I pray that he leaves.

Byron doesn't stop fucking me. His thrusts don't change at all, not faster or slower. He fucks me like he has forever—and he does. My father can't stop him. My father *won't* stop him.

One light, one heavy, one creak of his cane. My father's coming closer.

He must see me by now, must know what's happening. And yet he keeps walking nearer to us. He rounds the desk. *Light, heavy, creak.*

And stops.

"Sir?" Byron's breathing is heavy, the word clipped short. It's a parody of respect, the word *sir,* as he fucks the man's daughter over his desk. As his cock invades me, splitting me open.

"Byron." My father sounds tired and impossibly old. "Our documents. Look at them."

The documents are crushed in my hands. They are smeared with my mascara that smears across my cheek. They are ruined.

"Almost done," Byron says on a grunt.

I shiver from disgust, that my father is here watching this, that my fiancé doesn't seem to mind. I am something worse than a future wife or a beloved daughter. I am a pet, forced to beg and roll over for my dinner. And it's not even disgust at my father or at Byron that hollows out my stomach—it's disgust for myself. I let them do this to me. I don't fight. I can't fight. It's not only me who'll get hurt if I do.

A hand hovers over my head, shaking, trembling. Not Byron's hand. It's my father's.

He always shakes now. The doctors say it will only get worse. It started in his hand, then moved to his legs. That's when he started using the cane. He would have lost his life too. In his business any sign of weakness can be fatal. Competitors move in, take over. But no one

110

came to kill my father because Byron stepped in.

With my father's blessing, he'll take control of the family's businesses. His marriage to me will solidify the deal in the eyes of the more traditional mafiosos, smooth the way so less people fight it. And my father will get to live out his life in the empire he built, safe and sound and stroking the hair of his daughter as she gets fucked over his desk.

Every cell in my body revolts against his touch. But I remain still and outwardly calm. It's a skill I learned early in life—facing a monster and showing no fear.

I'm surrounded by monsters.

Byron grunts and digs his fingers into my flesh. He pulses inside me, and I know he's coming. *Finally.*

He pulls out with a wet sound. A warm swipe against my ass cheek quickly cools as he wipes his dick dry on me. The sound of a zipper fills the quiet room, then rustling as he puts himself to rights. My dress flips down.

As I lift my face, a piece of paper flutters back to the desk, unstuck from my cheek. My father strokes my hair one last time, and then his hand falls away. It feels like a strange ceremony has just taken place, the weight of it heavy in the air. The way a regular father would hand his daughter to her new husband at her wedding. But my father isn't normal. He's a Mafia don. The last in the line of the prestigious Moretti family. And he's given his blessing to the union.

I stand and catch myself on the desk before I fall. My legs are weak, like a baby deer struggling to hold myself up. It's Byron who pushes me up with a soft pat on my ass.

My father doesn't meet my eyes. Instead he busies himself straightening the papers on the desk.

Byron sits and gives me a bland smile. You'd never think he was inside me one minute ago. "Go back to the party. We have business to discuss." He pauses, then adds, "Enjoy yourself, darling."

We aren't in love. I hate him, and I think he might hate me too—for being born into the right family. Just with the wrong gender. If I'd been a man, I would have taken over the business in my own right. As it is, the other families require a man to lead, to respect. It's not only my cunt that keeps me docile, though. I don't have the heart to fight, to lead, to *kill* like they do.

Like Byron does. I'm terrified of him, but we'll be married in a matter of months.

Want to read more? Love The Way You Lie is available now at Amazon.com, iBooks, BarnesAndNoble.com and other retailers.

OTHER BOOKS BY SKYE WARREN

Standalone Dark Romance
Wanderlust
On the Way Home
His for Christmas
Hear Me

Stripped Series
Tough Love (prequel)
Love the Way You Lie
Better When It Hurts
Pretty When You Cry

Criminals and Captives Series
Prisoner

Dark Nights Series
Trust in Me
Don't Let Go

About the Author

Skye Warren is the New York Times and USA Today Bestselling author of dark romance. Her books are raw, sexual and perversely romantic.

Sign up for Skye's newsletter:
www.skyewarren.com/newsletter

Like Skye Warren on Facebook:
facebook.com/skyewarren

Join Skye Warren's Dark Room reader group:
skyewarren.com/darkroom

Follow Skye Warren on Twitter:
twitter.com/skye_warren

Visit Skye's website for her current booklist:
www.skyewarren.com

COPYRIGHT

Tough Love © 2015 by Skye Warren
Print Edition

Cover design by Book Beautiful
Cover photograph by Sara Eirew

Formatting by BB eBooks

Made in the USA
Columbia, SC
29 June 2022